Haboob

A novel by Anne Wilensky

Cartoons by Billy Stampone

A girl's journey thru the year 2012

Published by Haiku Helen Press

Published August 2012
© 2012 by Anne Pyne

Written, edited, and published by Anne Pyne

Drawings on front and back cover and inside book
by Bill Pyne aka Billy Stampone

cover designed by Helen Kritzler aka Haiku Helen

ISBN 978-0984097654
0984097651

Contact information: Willard Kraft
(520) 465-0999
5152 East 8th Street, Tucson, AZ 85711

First edition
Printed in the United States of America.

Thank you

A big thank you to everyone, I couldn't have
made it without you
All my love now and forever, Anne

Everyone is kind and helpful

And thank you to my angels
Bill Kraft, Frank Grijalva, Jack Schiro
and the girls at the credit union
I'm a lucky lass to have you as my friends...

You all make me happy..

All drawings inside book and on cover are by my husband Bill Pyne, aka Billy Stampone

Contents

Hello

Haboob is the tale of first half of year 2012 in one girl's life

Winter

The open road

Anne's friend Jim is teaching her to drive
He takes her to countryside outside Tucson to practice on
the open road..

Vince

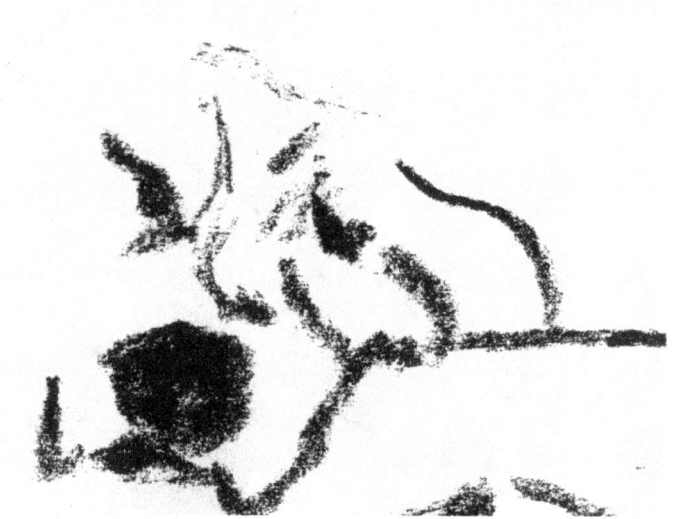

Our dog Skipper brought Vince to us

It is such a beautiful morning. Spring has started on the desert. There is nothing like it. The world is new born. The air is still chilly, the sound of birds chirping in their nest is everywhere. Perhaps they are sitting on their eggs. I don't know when the new babies are born.

O now the birds are calling to each other. There is nothing as thrilling as a bird call. They love calling to each other. It is like a high pitched whistle. And always comes from high up somewhere.

It is different from the chirping which is going on in the nests now. I don't know what the chirping is about. Maybe birds are just into conversation, they like talking to each other.

One little birdie is flying around now.

Yesterday was Sunday and since DMV is closed on Sunday, instead of practicing driving around town, Jim and I went to the DMV to practice the 3 point turn which is on the Drivers Test.

It wasn't easy. At first I made so many mistakes. Also I backed up too far and crashed into something.

So then I said "I'll drive you to the little street at edge of DMV and we can change seats."

I drove to edge of DMV where it meets that little road. And we both got out of truck to change seats so Jim could drive us to pool.

A man was walking across to the apartments on other side and we both said hi. But when I was standing up by the truck, he turned around and looked at me. "I know you," he said.

There was something familiar looking about him. "I

know you too," I said.

It turned out he was Vince. He worked for Chuck Rivett Fence Company. When Bill and I first moved into the house a car drove into the fence in backyard and knocked it down.

And the neighborhood children reported my dog Skipper was walking over the broken fence and getting out.

I called every fence company in town to ask them to come over and fix it right away and they all said "impossible!"

But when I called Chuck Rivett Fence, Vince answered and said he will send the men to do it this instant. Which he did. It meant so much to me. My dogs are my whole life. I didn't want Clio and Skipper able to walk out my backyard and go wherever they wanted.

Vince came over when the job was done so I could sign the paper for my house insurance. And he and Bill got along tremendously.

Vince is the nicest guy in the world. His passion then was for Muhammad Ali. There was a newspaper clipping with a photo of Vince holding up an award he had made for Muhammad Ali and saying why he is the greatest in all ways. It is from our local newspaper.

He asked Bill if he wanted a copy of it. It was a photocopy. And Bill really did want it. Vince got one from his car. And Bill actually framed it.

Vince is a talker and so enthusiastic and passionate and told Bill all about Muhammad Ali and how much he loves him and why.

Bill totally loved Vince. He loves people who are so outgoing, so friendly, and so warm. And he likes people who like to talk.

I think that is why Bill loved New York City so much. Everyone in New York City loves to talk. It is a city of big talkers.

We were not used to Tucson, the laconic West. Where people stay for only two seconds and say two words. Vince spent a whole hour here talking his head off and Bill loved him.

Two years later the flimsy wood fence between Caren's yard next door and our backyard was knocked over by wind. And huge Skipper was in her yard terrorizing her tiny little dog Pumpkin.

So I called Vince. And while his men worked to put up the strong chain link fence, I schmoozed with Vince in backyard. Bill was in art school then.

Five years later we called Vince again because we were going to try to put in fence in the front yard. So the dogs could go out there and watch the action on the street and keep us company in front yard.

But fence for the front yard is a huge project because it has to have a gate which opens and closes so Bill could bring the truck into the driveway.

Vince worked like a dog taking all the measurements, figuring out what would be best for us and estimating the cost.

But of course Vince being Vince, after all that hard work he stood around and schmoozed with us. We were all friends now and it was big love on all sides

Bill and I decided not to do that front yard fence. It was very expensive, beyond our means. It was too complicated with having a gate which automatically opens.

But Vince had knocked himself out to give us a good price. He told us he had started working for Chuck Rivett so many years ago, and Chuck had taught him you knock yourself out and go way out of your way to help the customer in any way. It was clearly a huge love between Vince and Chuck Rivett.

He had started there when he was so young and was

now the top man in charge of everything. He said how Chuck said "you are like a son to me and when he retires he wants Vince to manage the company."

I guess that was the last time we saw Vince. We had to have another small fence put in between Caren's driveway and our front yard.

So I called Vince. We had big love on the phone. And he sent over a guy who did the job in two hours.

The guy was great and I learned a great deal about chain link from him. He told me where he lived and said Vince had given him all the materials for free so he could put up a chain link fence all around his huge property way out in the desert.

And then I never saw or heard from Vince again until yesterday morning. When we both recognized each other.

Vince had been such a happy man when we first saw him and last saw him too. He had told me all about his TransAm and his personal license plate RIS. He says that stands for Real Italian Stallion. And he told me his son had got a license plate LIS.

"What's that?" he said to his son.

"Little Italian Stallion," his son said.

And Vince told me how passionate he is about tattoos

and showed me all his tattoos. He was just about the happiest man in the world. He was pleased as punch with his life.

He loved Chuck Rivett and working there. He told me about the posters he has up in his house. One of the beautiful blond TV star that Vince likes so much. (Linda Evans with her face like an angel.)

But instant we recognized each other yesterday (and he was on foot which surprised me, no one in Tucson is ever on foot) Vince told me all the catastrophes which had recently happened in his life.

Chuck Rivett had gone to Heaven, his son took over and instantly fired Vince after he had worked there 27 years.

Vince had run out of money, was homeless and was sleeping in his car. Then he had to give up his car. And was on food stamps.

At some point, I guess it was before he was evicted and sleeping in the park, he got so depressed he stayed home for 3 weeks without going out and without eating a morsel of food.

I think that is the first time he got out a big knife he had bought and it was less than a finger nail away from his stomach when they banged on his door. Someone had alerted the cops that something was wrong. And they took him to a help center or something. Maybe the hospital.

Then his parents both went to Heaven within a week of each other. He had to go to Kino Hospital all the time to see them, and when they went to Heaven he was devastated, he had been so close to them.

Maybe that is the second time he decided to kill himself. And then more bad stuff happened. And it was a third time he decided he couldn't take it.

He said now he has a place to live, he is living on 22nd Street and Craycroft, but no car, and he is on food stamps.

I said "can we give you a lift?" and he said no he is here visiting his friend. I guess he took the bus.

It was overwhelming. It was such a change from being on the top of the world, he had been so happy with his life, he loved everything about it.

He loved Chuck Rivett. He loved being the man in charge there. He loved his job. He loved his tattoos. He loved his Transam. He loved his personal license plate RIS (real Italian stallion). He loved his poster of the beautiful blond tv star. He loved every single thing about his life.

He loved getting a new tattoo every week. They were wild and when he took off his shirt to show me and Bill his brand new one, it covered his whole chest.

"I guess you hit bottom," I said when he finished up telling me everything with how close the knife was to his stomach. He showed me with his finger tips.

"Not this!" he said, making two inches.

"Not this!" he said making one inch.

"Not this!" he said making a tiny distance,

"But this!" he said bringing both fingers together.

I guess the knife was touching his body when they barged in and saved him.

"I hit bottom too," I said, "a few times, but at least I learned from it what mistakes not to make again."

I meant not to let myself get that upset.

But Vince misunderstood me. He said "I didn't make any mistakes, it was all done to me."

So I just said, "You've been thru a lot."

The amazing thing was our love. How much we loved each other, how much we hugged each other. How much love we expressed to each other.

I introduced him to Jim who was still in the drivers seat. He gave Jim such a warm handshake, Vince is warmest guy in the world. And said how happy he is to meet him.

And he told Jim wonderful things about me. "She is

such a warm loving open girl." And he thought about me many times remembering how nice I had been to him.

Since my new book was in back of the truck I offered Vince a copy. He was thrilled I had written a book.

"You wrote every word?" he said.

"Yes" I said.

He couldn't believe it was a gift, he thought I was showing it to him.

"It is for you" I said, and I got out my pen and wrote "For Vince, I love you."

He said he might not read it, not all of it (I keep forgetting how many people don't enjoy reading). But he said he will cherish it and hold on to it forever.

I said "you can look at the cartoons, I put in Bill's cartoons."

Then I told him about Bill. I thought it might help him to know he isn't alone in having huge difficult things happen in his life out of the blue.

Maybe I should not have told him, because it was such a drag for me. Vince wouldn't let me off the hook, kept pressing me for details.

There just are no details. It was Bill's time, period. The decision was made by Heaven with agreement by Bill's soul, and that is all there is to it.

Not that anyone believes me on this.

Believe me if it were anyone but Vince, I would have been annoyed with them if they kept pressing me for details, and wouldn't let me off the hook, and kept using the words "die," "died."

I did finally say "I don't like the word died, I like going to Heaven."

He instantly changed to "passed," but it was a topic I could not get out of.

It didn't touch in any way my deep profound love for Vince, and the huge love which passed between us in the DMV parking lot yesterday morning.

Then Vince finally said, "I said how wonderful and warm you are just now. I take it back. Like Ali, you are the greatest."

Which is the highest compliment in the world because Muhammad Ali is the person Vince loves more than anyone in the world.

And then we had a huge hug again. And I got back in the truck.

And then Jim and I went to the pool and when I got home, I lied in bed in front of the TV and did not budge for long time.

My experience with Vince was a huge experience for me. Who would ever have imagined I had that much love for my fenceman. It was as much love as the Pacific Ocean. Bigger than that. Bottomless and infinite in all directions.

"My husband loved you so much" I said to Vince.

And that is true.

January 16

Divine Driving Lesson Yesterday

Time for new shoes

I hadn't done any driving since New Years Day when we did big driving in town, on Glen Road, which Jim says is cheating since it is a back road thru town, not a major street.

I like it tho, because there is no stress of traffic, but so many lights and 4 ways stops that I get to practice a lot.

Yesterday to lift my spirits and get back in the swing of driving, we went to Corona Road way out in the countryside.

It was heaven. LOL the first two weeks of this new year were no picnic for me. It was like life used me for a punching bag.

By yesterday morning I was down but not out! Driving really did save me. I am falling in love with it. Because yesterday's driving was glorious.

We stopped and got gas on the way and Jim washed my windshield for me exquisitely. That is the kind of thing Bill would do for me. Bill didn't mind work and liked to do things right. And liked to help me, he was my husband.

Jim is a friend, which means he does the things I don't know how to do yet. He puts the gas in the truck but he sits behind the wheel while I wash the windshield.

But on the way to the countryside, instead of keeping

the bad feelings I had for the previous 3 nights private, I confided them to Jim as he was driving.

My wonderful dog Beanie, had gone to Heaven suddenly out of nowhere the week before.

Jim knew about it and I am sure he worried about me the first few days afterwards. But miraculously I had seemed to bounce back very fast.

And almost immediately after that I had to register both my cars and take them both to emissions. There was so much I had to do, and Jim drove both cars to emissions for me.

We did both in one morning. And during the long wait each time I had fun teasing him. And the previous Sunday we had bet on football, and I had a stunning win and I was bragging a lot. So both of us assumed I had weathered everything fine.

But then 4 nights ago, I started waking up in middle of night with bad thoughts. I just hit bottom.

The days were fine, but the nights were bad.

Which is why I really wanted to do driving yesterday morning. I wanted to break out of the gloom which was coming to me at night.

So I told Jim the bad thoughts I had as we were driving

to countryside. I think it scared him, he has never seen me unhappy. And it was easy to tell him about the bad thoughts because I was happy in the car on the way to go driving.

I was excited about it. And very happy to be out of town and in the countryside.

I think this is why he washed the windshield so exquisitely for me, which I appreciated so much. He wanted to help me and bring back all my happiness. And it worked.

After that an upswing started which just grew and grew. Instead of waiting till we got to Corona Road to switch seats, when we got to the road which leads into that whole area and he said "there's not a car on the road."

I said "Why don't I start driving now. If it's too hard we can always switch back. Let me give it a shot."

And I was driving so happily, so confidently and so well, I was so happy that I started kidding around.

I said "losing my husband and my dog sure does wonders for my driving."

He said "but you wouldn't be driving if you hadn't lost Bill."

I said "that's true, but losing my dog sure bumped it up

a notch."

I was giggling because I knew it was the best driving I had ever done. I actually was at whole new level.

And then I was home free and so was Jim. It was losing Beanie which had brought on the dark thoughts. And once I was joking and kidding around about it behind the wheel I was free.

I can't explain it, it was as if the gloom turned into a tiny white feather and just floated away. And all turned into ecstasy.

I have no explanation for anything. I have no idea why that gloom arrived 3 nights in a row, and why it suddenly transformed into ecstasy when I got behind the wheel.

It was a heavenly driving lesson. When it was all over and we were heading back to town, I said to Jim, "it was a divine driving lesson." And it was.

First I drove us to our country favorite road, Swan Road. It was so interesting and beautiful, that stormy sky and desert on both sides. And I was so completely relaxed. I was driving with one hand.

It just seemed like driving took no effort of any kind.

It was warmer than I thought and I wanted the air on my shoulders, so Jim held the wheel while I peeled off my blouse and pulled my skirt up to turn it into a halter dress.

LOL he had to hold the wheel and steer and look away at the same time because there was a minute of being topless involved.

But there was no other car on the road. And Jim is such a genius driver he can steer the wheel from the passenger seat with his eyes closed.

I am always peeling off shirts as I am driving but usually I have a slip underneath, this is the first time I was naked on Corona Road.

I actually can now drive and take off my top layers at the same time. But I wasn't able to navigate driving, pulling off my blouse, and pulling up my skirt to cover my top, all at the same time.

So after that was accomplished and the lovely air was blowing all over my naked shoulders and I was so happy, I teased Jim, "Don't worry I won't do that with my driving examiner during my driving test."

He is obsessed with my do's and don'ts during my driving test.

For instance when I stop at a stop sign at an intersection, Jim likes me to nose out a little so I can see the cars coming in both directions, he trained me to do that. But he said during my driving test I am not to do that. I am to stop exactly at the stop sign.

There so many do's and don'ts he tells me that I have stopped paying attention. Instead all I do now is tease him about my driving test.

"Don't worry" I said, "I won't get naked during my driving test."

It was such a breeze driving the long road in country to dead end with my bare shoulders in the sweet air and the driving so automatic for me.

And then we passed the bulls on the side of the road. 5 magnificent bulls lying down resting by the side of the road, one with a calf nestled by him.

So I pulled over and sweet talked one of them for quite a while. For almost 5 minutes I called out endearments. He twitched his ear in response. He was listening.

Then we saw ravens circling overhead, I loved that. I identified with them, I knew I was looking at my freedom and my happiness.

When we got back to where we started I said "I'm going to do it again."

But Jim said "there is a turn off, let's turn off that and explore." He knows how much I love to explore.

And it turned out to be a road he was never on, so it was interesting for him too. It was a dirt road and for some reason I am very talented at driving on dirt roads. I don't find it fun, it is such a bumpy ride. But Jim likes it so much that I am good at it, it means something to him.

And then again, a miracle. Jim said "Look!" And again 5 bulls lying down by side of road. I didn't stop this time. But I went as slow as I could to drink in the sight.

I have fallen in love with bulls now. Jim kept hoping he'd spot a coyote for me but I was happy with bulls.

Then after a long time the dirt road became paved. And of course a paved road is such a treat after the dirt road which is being bumped around all the time.

That came to what looked like a big road. I turned on the big road. There were no cars and it did not go very far, turned into a little road.

And then finally I decided "OK I am willing to return to town."

I hadn't wanted my ride in the countryside to end. I thought returning to town meant returning to my dull life, and I liked everything being thrilling, new, and wonderful.

It was impossible to see the turn off back to the dirt road to return. No one but Jim could have seen it. I overshot it and tried to do a U turn to get back to it. Cars were coming as I was stretched across the road.

The dirt road didn't seem so bumpy on the return trip. And there were my wonderful bulls again and I drove really slow to drink them in.

And when I got to the light I said "OK I'm ready to go back," and switched seats.

And I glowed all the way home about my divine driving lesson.

"You did good," he said.

"It was a divine driving lesson," I said.

We stopped for breakfast burritos as soon as we hit town. Such a sweet Mexican man at the drive-thru counter. That warm happy face and warm happy smile

And I knew my happiness was so solid that the bad thoughts would not return in the evening and during the night.

I had turned a corner. And it is true my happiness held.

I had sweet sleep and constructive dreams all night.

In my dream everything which needed to be taken care of got taken care of perfectly.

I guess driving saved me when I needed to be saved.

January 18

Noshing on life...

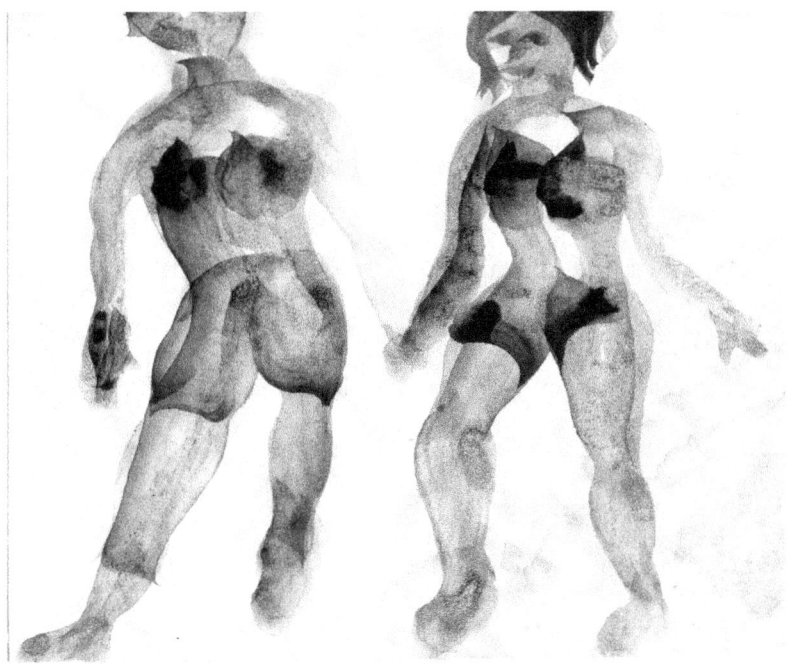

Dancers

It is an intense time but I am getting addicted to it. I'm beginning to see an intense time means all is intense. As if the artist changed the colors on his palette. In this case life is the artist. The beauty is far more intense. The colors of sky and nature out my window are far more vivid. Deeper, clearer, more beautiful.

Maybe intense means more alive. This intense time waltzed in the day after New Years Day, on January 2nd, and put us all thru the ringer for two weeks.

We had stormy seas, we had shipwreck, everything which could happen did happen. Our worst nightmares came to pass.

And yet here we are in safe harbor again. Altho probably on another shore. We must have crossed over some big divide. Because we have landed and the world is filled with incredible beauty.

It is a fresh new, brand new beauty, and the color and the beauty are far more vivid. A beauty extraordinaire! Colors extraordinaire!

And cat on my windowsill looking out. Sitting on my windowsill by the open window. My Priscilla.

O my Priscilla, my wonderful Priscilla, my cat extraordinaire.

O here comes her husband! He was sleeping on the chest by the other open window. She didn't see him wake up. She didn't see him creep over both file cabinets and around my

desk. And onto the windowsill which opens to backyard. He
wanted to get out.

Her husband is the huge alley cat from across the way
who seems to have taken up residence in my house. He
sleeps here now. And he arrives to eat Priscilla's food and
her daughter's food.

It's hard to call Muggles Priscilla's husband tho,
because of his bad behavior. He beats up all their children,
they all finally left, only Cupcake remained. And his hobby
used to be trying to beat up Priscilla and Cupcake too.

She didn't see him coming, I did. But when he reached
out his huge paw to touch her— all in one motion she
turned around, hissed, snarled, and leaped up into the tree.

He terrorizes his family. I really did make an all-out
effort to evict him from the yard and the house, but he won.
He spends all his nights here now and he steals their food.

Priscilla is sitting high up in the tree right now. I can see
her thru the open window. She is watching me type and I
am watching her in the crook of the tree.

The whole constellation of my house has changed now
that my dog Beanie went to Heaven two weeks ago.

Now it is just me and the kitties. Me and Priscilla and
Cupcake. I don't count Muggles, he is not a pet. He is a

scoundrel who sleeps here, and helps himself to their food.

So now Priscilla is sitting up there in the crick of the tree, looking at me, and I am looking at her. She is part of my landscape looking out my window. I love it! My life has come down to Priscilla and me and Cupcake too.

3 bachelorettes sharing a home together. Sharing a bed at night, sharing a house, sharing a yard.

The big shake-out over the past two weeks happened and that is where it is now. How the new life shaped up. The new start. The new big adventure. We are all still getting used to brand new regime.

And none of us knows what will happen next.

I have never lived life without any predictability at all. The last support of predictability in my life was Beanie. Priscilla and Cupcake don't give my life predictability. They are my companions in unpredictability.

I never experienced life this way, having no idea minute to minute, day by day, what life is going to bring me. I never had that attitude about life.

It is as if life is a banquet or I am in a restaurant and the waiters arrive carrying food for the patrons. And none of us knows which food they will bring us. Different dishes keep coming out.

Some I like, some I don't like. The only thing which seems for sure is one dish is whisked away and another different one arrives.

Did you ever hear of such a thing? Spending my life noshing on the banquet of life?

That's really what I'm doing now, noshing on life. Whatever the waiter happens to bring me I nosh on it, whatever it is. And I have no idea what it is and what is coming next.

January 30th

Spying at the DMV

A lot goes on at the DMV

Julie, the lifeguard at the Y, said they didn't make her parallel park for her road test, instead they made her do a 3 point turn. She said before she took the test she went there to spy.

The person had to drive on 22nd Street, then turn off into a neighborhood, then around the neighborhood, and then back to the DMV. Then they had to do a 3 point turn instead of parallel park.

So on Thursday Jim and I went to the DMV on 22nd Street, instead of the one on Alvernon, to spy.

Jim couldn't figure out what Julie meant by a 3 point turn, and even tho Samantha at the desk of the Y drew a diagram of what you have to do at DMV, he couldn't figure out the diagram.

So we went there and we both watched it. It was a lady in a big white truck. I couldn't understand what I was watching but Jim understood, so we will practice it.

While she was doing it he said "she got herself in trouble." Also he said "she didn't leave herself enough room, and her mistake was..."

I didn't get any of it, but when he followed them for the driving, I understood everything perfectly. Altho 22nd Street is a huge street, I saw her creep along in the slow lane (I can do that!) and then turn right into a neighborhood.

Jim thought we weren't allowed to be spying, so kept

big distance, so we almost lost them in the neighborhood. But by some miracle Jim figured out where they went and found them again.

I really don't think I will have any trouble with driving this route, I just have to remember to stop at all the stop signs.

Saturday I am spaced

Far out!

But when we went to Mervyns parking lot for me to get reversing, the 3 point turn is all about reversing, I simply couldn't get how to turn the wheel so the back of the truck would go in the direction I want.

I had been incredibly spaced out for the whole previous week. I have no idea why. I am convinced now there must have been a major frequency change.

I think by Saturday morning it had finally completed

itself. It began the day after New Years. It lasted for almost 4 weeks. A lot of stuff happened to a lot of people including me during it.

But when I woke up Saturday morning I knew the whole thing had completed itself. The only problem was I was in a totally altered state.

I couldn't find my mind for love or money. While Jim was driving us to Mervyns he said something to me in the car.

I said "I can tell you are talking, I know you must be saying words, but that is as far as I can get."

After that he didn't try to talk to me, and I kept saying "far out!" at everything we passed.

I was just looking out the window and saying "far out!"

I wasn't seeing anything we were passing. I was just expressing my state of mind.

I said "far out" about 11 times on the way to Mervyns.

He didn't say another word to me when he found out language was beyond me.

I said "I don't know why you're not in an altered state too. I bet we are in the 4th Dimension now."

LOL I think he smoked a joint before he picked me up. "Well that probably grounded you" I said, "else you'd be in altered state like me."

I really do think I was way further out than any pot could take you.

To Alice's house we go

But the next day I was solid as a rock. Whatever the huge January transition was, I think it is over.

I said "take me to Glen Road and I'll drive on that."

He said "why don't you drive us there Annie, it's just a few miles down Craycroft, you can do it."

Craycroft is a huge street. I was tense the whole way but I did it!

And we arrived on Glen. I instantly relaxed.

I really did drive Glen well. Lots of red lights, lots of 4 way stops, and driving across huge intersections. But I was comfortable with all of it, I really was a confident driver.

And of course I amused myself the whole way by teasing Jim.

I said "OK I'll drive you to Alice's house, you can have your roast chicken."

This is a huge joke for me. On New Years Day Alice invited us both for roast chicken. Neither of us wanted to go, we just wanted to do driving and go for swim at his club.

But Alice really wanted us to come. The more I said we had planned to have a different day, the more she said we could come for roast chicken. Finally I succeeded in making her understand.

But for the next 10 days I lied to Jim.

"I got email from Alice, she wants to know when you are showing up for your roast chicken."

I can't believe he fell for that! He actually turned off his phone (he is not on email) so Alice would not make him show up for roast chicken. Jim loves Alice and would not hurt her feelings.

So naturally yesterday I said "I'm driving you to Alice's house for your roast chicken.

"But I am not driving you for free. You have to pay me!

"It is the same as taxi cab in NYC. $1.35 for first 1/5th of mile, and then 20 cents for each 1/5th of mile after that.

"And if you don't want me to leave you stranded there, you have to pay for the return trip too.

"Plus I expect a nice tip."

I can't believe he falls for all my nonsense. He kept protesting that after all the times he has driven me, why does he have to pay me to be driven to Alice's house.

And he was mad that I expected a big tip to boot.

"I hope you brought your wallet" I said, "this is not going to be cheap."

But I hadn't bothered switching to 3rd gear one of the times while I was driving, so I was not able to step on it fast enuf to make the light and it was such a long light.

"My mistake!" I said.

He said "I'm deducting 5 dollars from the taxi ride."

"No you don't!" I said, "you can take it off my tip.

"Call Alice on your cell," I said, "tell her I am bringing you for your roast chicken."

I can't believe he believed me. When we reached bottom of Glen, he said "this is the turn off to Alice's house."

I said "we're not going to Alice's."

I was hungry and just wanted to go home and eat. So we

switched places and he drove us home.

"You can take any route you want," I said.

So when we got stuck at that long light, he just made right turn on red, and took a different fast route home thru major boulevards.

And for some reason I was walking on air. I just felt glorious. It was such a beautiful day, such gorgeous sunshine. It was heaven being driven by Jim, he is such expert driver, and just to totally relax and be totally happy. I felt glorious.

I said "What a great driving lesson! I loved every instant of it! What a great morning! What a perfect morning! I'm so happy. And I love being happy. Nothing makes me happier than being happy."

I didn't even tease him on the way home, I was too happy to tease. I just kept wriggling with joy and saying how happy I am.

February 5th

To the rez for cigs..

The plan had been to go on Saturday when DMV is closed to practice the 3 point turn there, but when Saturday came I was too out of it to want to drive. The most I thought I could manage is going swimming.

It was not a major out-of-it like the previous Saturday, it was more like zero energy. When I had woken up Saturday morning, the only thing which had appealed to me was staying in bed all day and sleeping on and off. It was that kind of day.

Which seemed so inexplicable because the week had begun off gangbusters. It had been such a high energy week. But I guess on Friday it turned around.

So when Jim called yesterday morning about driving, I said "I'm out of it, just drive me to the Indian reservation for my cigarettes, then let's swim, and come straight home and watch TV."

He's always glad when I don't want to go somewhere after swimming so he can be home with his cat and watch his scary movies on TV.

Even being driven to the Indian reservation seemed to require energy, I have no idea why. It's not really that I was out of it, it was more like I just wasn't there.

I woke up when he saw the long long line for cigarettes and started to curse.

He hates waiting patiently on long lines.

I was going to try to sweet talk him thru the wait but luckily he got a call on his cell phone. So I just looked out the window and connected to my Higher Self.

He perked up from the call on his cellphone, but it was someone asking him for a favor which he really did not want to do and did not know how to get out of. I guess compared with having to do that, waiting on line didn't seem so bad.

And then it was our turn. I wanted to buy a lot of cartons of cigs so I wouldn't have to make Jim drive me again for a long time, but the man said he just doesn't have them on hand, and next time call ahead of time and he will have them.

The Indian who waited on us was so absolutely lovely in every way, it brightened both of our spirits. I think Jim was in another world too, altho he wouldn't admit it.

We drove to swimming pool in same daze we had driven to rez for cigarettes.

But my swim was totally lovely, the water was so warm and lovely. I loved it.

The next day the lady who takes water aerobics before I arrive for my swim told me she had been at her credit union on Saturday morning.

Her teller was taking a long time to look up her account.

So she noticed all the way down at the other end was a girl who had very curly hair which looked just like mine.

She was wondering if it was me, when the girl actually robbed the bank.

I couldn't wait for Jim to arrive to pick me up.

"When the police question you, remember to tell them I was at the rez buying cigarettes, and then went swimming and then came home and didn't budge.

"That's our story and we're sticking to it!

"Also tell the police I only have Learners Permit, I would never rob the Federal Credit Union without a licensed driver sitting next to me."

I told him what Marilyn said and at first he got serious. "The police think you did it?" he asked.

"It couldn't have been you" he said, "you won't drive on 22nd Street."

"Good thinking!" I said, "be sure to tell the police that.

"I'd never drive to Federal Credit Union, stick up the bank, and make a fast getaway with just a Learners Permit."

He said "You can't make a fast getaway, it takes you 20 minutes to figure out where the clutch is."

La Bandita

Birthday letter to my brother

I write letter to my brother on his birthday

Label is my dad's given name, many Jewish boys were named Label then. They all changed it to American names when they grew up. Most to Larry or Louis, they probably wanted to be baseball players and chose a name a ball player had back then.

But my dad was reading Emma Bovary, her lover was named Leon. He chose Leon for himself. Label aka Leon was always a romantic.

Hi Jimmy,

The day you were born I was in Kulla Kindergarten on the ground floor of Grandma's building.

A lady came in from the office and spoke to my teacher and my teacher said "Annie you are not to go home, instead take the elevator upstairs to your grandmother's apartment.

"You will be staying with her. Your mother is in the hospital having her baby."

I found out when I was older that Leon was proctoring a Regents exam when he got the call you were born.

I know now you were born at 3:30 in the afternoon. I must have already been upstairs in Grandma's house when you were actually born.

I had to stay with Grandma till Mommy came home from the hospital with you.

I'd take the elevator down to school in the morning and back up to Grandma's house on the 6th floor when school was over.

Grandma made me breakfast in the morning.

One morning, maybe it was after a weekend, both Grandma and I forgot about school.

We had our breakfast together, I sat at the table while she washed the dishes.

Then she sat down with her coffee and we played cards.

We were very happy together. It was so peaceful.

Then the doorbell rang and the lady from nursery school burst in.

"Mrs. Geller why isn't Annie in school!"

It was an awful way to have our peace interrupted.

I didn't like school, I liked being with Grandma, and the lady seemed so loud.

And so bossy!

I had to go right downstairs to school.

I knew Mommy was having the baby, I was thrilled, I wanted a baby with all my heart. I wanted a sister so I could have a live-in best friend.

I kept asking God for a sister.

Maybe I was at Grandma's house for a week. Leon had to show up for dinner. I don't know if he wanted to.

His wife was in the hospital, his daughter was at his mother's house, it was the first time since he was married that he was free, and did not have to come right home after work.

Maybe he wanted to meet his friends after work, maybe

he would have preferred to go out to dinner with them.

But he had no choice he had to show up at his mother's house for dinner.

Grandma doted on him. I sat in the kitchen with her for 2 hours while she prepared his dinner. She was lost in a wave of happiness. She would murmur to me the whole time about him "Label this and Label that."

I didn't pay attention. Only when she said "Annela go to the frigidaire and get me the..."

The frigidaire was on the other side of the kitchen, far from the stove and where she was preparing for cooking his meal.

One evening he was late. We sat in the kitchen and waited and waited and waited.

Finally the doorbell rang. "Annela" she said, "go to the door and let your father in."

I opened the door to him. "You're late" I said.

"Is she mad?" he asked, "the subways were murder."

It was such conspiratorial whispering at the door.

He was so beautiful and handsome and did not seem like a father. He acted like a mother's son who was in trouble with his mother.

I must have been there while he ate dinner, but everyone

ignored me. Grandma only had eyes for him. And he was paying a lot of attention to his mother.

I found it very relaxing to be there and be ignored, to be a bystander.

It was the high point of our day when Leon arrived for dinner. Not so much for me because I was ignored, but for Grandma. Who prepared for it and waited for it for two hours and was in bliss when it happened. She glowed.

She loved having her son home, he was the apple of her eye.

Even tho I was only 4 and a half years old when I opened the door to him when he was so late, and he said "is she mad, the subways were murder," I knew from his excitement and his handsomeness, and because he acted like I was a little sister, not his daughter, I knew he had been having fun with his friends and forgotten all about his family.

I found it all exciting and interesting.

On the weekend he picked me up to visit Mommy in the hospital, I am sure you were already born.

I know now it was Flower 5th Avenue Hospital. Which is on 5th Avenue and 106th Street. All I remember is he stopped at the little store in the lobby to buy perfume for

Mommy. I don't know why I don't remember seeing Mommy or you.

Is it possible children were not allowed? My big thrill and interest was him buying the perfume for Mommy.

I found that tremendously romantic.

And then finally I was allowed to be taken home after nursery school, instead of going back up in the elevator to Grandma's house.

And I walked in the door, and there in my room, my friend Richie was holding you on a pillow.

And I was overcome by rage and jealousy. I flew into the room, grabbed you on the pillow out of his arms, and screamed at him "you have no right to hold my new baby before me."

Mommy was there, Richie's mother Beverly, and Richie. They were all sitting on 3 chairs together.

Mommy was totally embarrassed that I was yelling at my best friend in a rage.

And would not give up holding you on the pillow, he had done such a sin by holding you first. I was shocked out of my mind when I saw what was going on behind my back.

So Beverly and Richie had to go back downstairs to their

apartment.

I wasn't willing to share you with Richie.

Well Jimmy I guess you had a tempestuous big sister.

You sure were a wonderful little brother tho.

And our closeness as children was a constant joy and happiness in my life.

I love you.

Happy Birthday.

Your sister Annie

Happy Birthday Jimmy

March is intense

March 11

Jim and I have a fight

"It's your fault I crashed into it!"

Well I have to take my first road test in a month, that is when Learners Permit expires, else I will have to take the written test again.

However I only have to take my first road test before April 10th (the date on my learners permit). After that I have a whole year long to take my 2nd and 3rd road test.

Which means I don't have to pass road test before April 10th but have to be prepared to take it.

I didn't know that, I thought I had to pass the test by April 10th or take written test all over again. I just found out.

So we are still working on the 3 point turn.

Last weekend instead of practicing it, Jim took me out to Corona Road in the countryside so I could be behind the wheel and drive again in beautiful countryside.

I really needed that because the week before we had tried to practice the 3 point turn every morning because I put pressure on myself to speed up learning it in time for the test. That is when I thought I had to pass it by April 10th.

The pressure and speed-up in learning turned out to be big mistake. I crashed into the fireplug on corner of my yard and did big damage to truck and knocked out one of the rear lights.

I was very mad at Jim after that. I was shocked at how much damage I had done.

But it is water under the bridge now. It upset him terribly when I was so mad at him about it. And it upset me terribly being so mad at Jim.

Ours is really a beautiful friendship. And altho I'm used to having emotions in my friendships with girlfriends. Or emotions with my husband. Or boyfriends before I was with Bill. I never in my whole life had emotions enter the picture with a boy who is just a friend.

That is the beautiful thing about a friendship with a boy, emotions don't go on.

It is just about enjoying each others companionship.

So it knocked us both for a loop that I was so mad at him. It upset me terribly being mad at him and upset him very much too.

It took me a whole week to calm down from it.

But last Saturday he suggested we go to Corona Road. He knows how happy that makes me. I hadn't done any actual driving in long time, it had been all about the 3 point turn.

But it turned out to be ideal. There was not another car on the road, and the beauty was breath-taking.

The blue of the sky was the most beautiful blue I ever saw. Not that deep deep blue which I thought was my favorite, but a soft blue.

Not turquoise because there was no green in it. It was flawless blue and such a lovely shade.

And the mountains too were so beautiful against it with their blue charcoals and hints of purple.

And I got a glimpse of 3 coyote pups as they crossed the road and dashed off. They were very small.

And Jim kept pointing out to me the hawks circling above, and I saw the red of their back feathers.

And a posse of cows lying down, which ambled off when I approached.

At the end I went a little distance on a dirt road, where the view of sky and mountains was so beautiful I almost cried from the beauty.

That is when I hit bliss, and that is when both Jim and I knew I was all right again.

I was in such ecstasy drinking in that beauty that I was just up there in a plateau of bliss.

Jim looked at me and said, "you're all right again?"

I said "yes."

LOL I think he was relieved.

And after that we went back to being friends as we had been. Our happiness in our friendship was restored. We were relaxed with each other again. And had fun together again.

Now that it is a week later, I don't think it is such a bad thing we had that falling out. Even tho it upset both of us so badly at the time.

Because a friendship is a relationship too, and all relationships want to grow. A big shake-out like that causes a clean slate when things are working again.

You don't return to the same place, you are on a higher exponent it seems to me. Awareness of each other is greater so we can get to know each other better.

Yesterday we went back to Mervyns parking lot to practice the 3 point turn again. And Jim said I was a lot better at it.

Altho I don't know how to straighten up when I am in reverse. I still have to learn that. But for the first time since the fight, my sense of humor came back while I was driving with Jim.

It was fun teasing him and making him laugh. And he has been teasing me about the purple wildflower which came up in my yard. It is at the end of my driveway.

So I always want him to be very careful when he pulls out to take me swimming. So of course he always says he is aiming for it to run it over.

It's a good joke on me. But not as funny as the dirty remark I made during the 3 point turn in Mervyns parking lot yesterday. It was so much fun to shock the pants off Jim.

I was such a good girl with my husband and he was my main companion in Tucson for the whole 20 years we were here, that it really tickles me to be naughty with Jim.

All I can say is it is a lot of fun to be friends with a boy who is just a friend and not a boyfriend. Because of the freedom. It's fun to feel so free. And so relaxed.

O well it's Sunday, I guess I will have to drive in town today and get used to being in traffic again. I haven't done this for a month. I will just do Glen Road.

If I have energy afterwards Jim wants us to go over to DMV and practice the 3 point turn there. Oy gevalt!

Jim's Yiddish is becoming superb. We were at the Jewish bakery on Purim and I bought him a Hamentashen.

I said, "today is Purim, that's how you celebrate Purim, you eat a hamentashen."

I got myself chocolate éclair but I made Jim eat his hamentashen. But he liked it!

March 24th

My mother and me

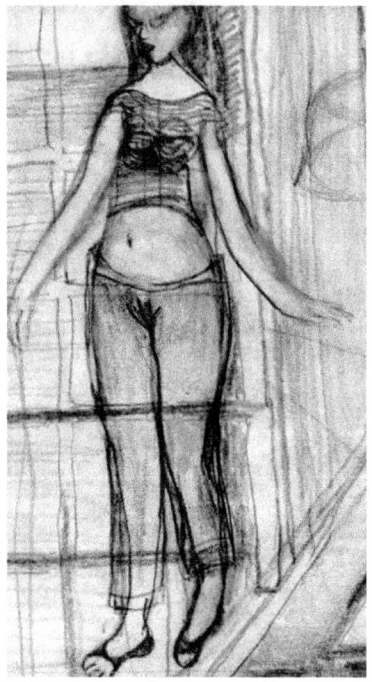

A daughter's story

Katy and I did Higher Self together on the telephone yesterday afternoon. We had not done it for a year.

Yesterday Katy called me as soon as she opened her eyes or when she was first getting up. But because of the time difference it was noon for me and I had just that instant arrived back from swim pool.

Actually I think I was lying outside in the sunshine smoking a cigarette when the phone rang. I hadn't gone in yet to look at what I had cooking on the stove. I was about to when phone rang.

Altho I thought "it's not a good time, I was starving hungry whole time in pool and I was just about to prepare food."

We talk on the phone a lot when she is helping me with my book. But the rest of the time it is usually once a month, she calls me for a reason. Ever since she first began writing about 6 months ago she would call when she wrote something new to try it out on me.

This is quite a treat for me. Katy was an artist her whole life, but writing is brand new. It comes from a very deep very real place. I feel let into her world when she reads it to me on the phone. I like it.

But the first thing she said was "I just woke up," so I knew it wasn't because she just finished writing a piece. She was calling to talk.

First she politely asked about me but I knew that wasn't why she was calling. So I didn't get sidetracked talking about me, answered briefly and then said "tell me all about you."

She said "the good news is I have two new friends," and she told me all about them.

"But I am also having problems." And she told me her two problems.

After she finished telling me, my Higher Self suggested "Ask her if she wants to do Higher Self."

Katy has had zero interest in doing Higher Self together for almost whole of past year, but this time to my surprise she said "that is a good idea."

"Let me go to the bathroom and I will call you right back," she said.

"Perfect!" I said, "I will go to where my cigarettes are all set up for myself."

Actually I did have cigarettes outside, but the sun had too much heat in it, I wanted to go indoors.

I went to my back bedroom but instead of facing the TV, I faced looking out the open window and put my cigs right next to me.

The way we do Higher Self together on the phone, is we both tune into our Higher Self at same time. I ask the questions and she repeats what her Higher Self says.

The first thing her Higher Self said was "This is for both Anne and Katy. There is a new world going on out there, and the reason you girls are having problems is because problems are the only thing which motivate you to open that door and walk out into the brand new world.

"Otherwise you just stay where you are."

Then the phone went dead in the middle of a sentence. I stayed where I was for about 5 minutes, then figured Katy will call me back and went to my stove.

I spent about 20 minutes. I was involved in cooking which is a new thing for me.

I took a bowl of vegetable stew and went back to bed in front of open window and ate it. Just then Katy called.

She was filled with apologies, it had been an emergency she had to help someone. But she didn't need to apologize. It had been the perfect time for me to deal with all the stuff cooking on my stove.

So we tuned into our Higher Self again, and this time to my surprise, Katy's Higher Self began saying right away about our mothers. Both our mothers are in Heaven now, altho Katy's Higher Self called it "the spirit world."

And she said both Katy and I have problems in our life now because we still hold it against our mothers the stuff our mothers did which shocked and upset us.

"Anne discovered right after Eleanor went to Heaven that her mom had disinherited her. And Katy because when she returned home from college with the great love of her life, her mother seriously acted up because he was a black revolutionary."

Katy's Higher Self explained to both of us:

"For a mother, raising a child is everything, it is their whole life. They want more than anything else for their child to be safe, they put that above everything else.

"Your mothers bought into what was believed back then, the right way to raise your child and the wrong way.

"And when something you did freaked them out, that they thought would lead to disaster for their child. That their child would wind up homeless destitute on the street, on drugs.

"Then they resorted to force to try to get you to stop what they called doing something wrong and to do it right.

Force wasn't really at their disposal, Katy and I were grown up, but they were willing to be harsh.

Katy's Higher Self said, "they would have done anything, even keep you in a cage, to stop you from what they thought was doing the wrong thing.

"Because keeping you safe was everything to them, even if it ruined the relationship."

She also said, "The reason Eleanor spent her whole life trying to control Anne is because she did not have control over herself.

"She never found balance, so she tried to keep too tight a hold on herself and as a result too tight a hold over Anne.

"But Anne always broke her mother's rules, which is why the relationship had so much conflict. Why Eleanor always behaved in a way which upset Anne so much.

"But Eleanor simply freaked out when Anne would not do what Eleanor and her generation believed was the right thing to do.

"It frightened Lillian for Katy's safety that she did not marry, did not have children, did not have a career.

"And it frightened Eleanor for Anne's safety that she wasn't going to work."

Katy's Higher Self explained that "because of our mothers' behavior to us, we withheld love from our mothers, and this is causing us both problems right now."

She said "it is causing problems for your mothers in the spirit world too. They feel guilty."

"And the only way Anne and Katy can give their

mothers all the love which will set them free, and set Katy and Anne free too, is instead of seeing them as their mothers, but seeing them as their little daughters.

"A little girl who is frightened and confused and needs a lot of love. Just love and nothing but love. That will set everyone free."

She felt the pattern was set deep in the past.

"Eleanor's behavior and feelings came from her relationship with her mother. And her mother was harsh and mean because of her relationship with her mother.

"That Eleanor was a frightened little girl because her mother was harsh and mean. And then Anne became frightened when Eleanor was harsh and mean when she panicked about something Anne was doing."

Whew!!! What a mess!!

But the solution is simple. "Just see them as little girls now, see them as frightened little girls, who need lots of love. Love love and nothing but love.

"Overlook their problems the way you would if you had a little daughter. You would just want to love her, and give her the love which would make her know everything is OK."

It all had a deep impact on me.

Altho for the past week to my surprise I have been remembering nice things my mother did. Still when she tries to connect with me from Heaven, I refuse to be in relationship with her. I have closed my heart to her.

I would have overlooked everything else if there had not been the shock of discovering a week after she went to Heaven that she had disinherited me.

Even yesterday afternoon right after the phone call, when I set about changing my tune and loving my mother, it came so fast into my mind, how much she must have hated me to have disinherited me.

My whole life she had acted like she didn't like me but Katy's Higher Self said that wasn't true.

"It had nothing to do with you, that was all about her trying to control you because she did not have control over herself, that was all about holding on with too tight a grip."

I can get over everything which took place when I was a daughter under her roof, but I still have not gotten over seeing her disinheriting me as an expression of pure hatred. It's not about the money.

But I had made it absolutely clear to her several years before that she can't control me, I won't let her.

I had done this because my Higher Self said it was for

her. "That when her husband went to Heaven, she needed a real relationship with her daughter. And the only way to have that, a relationship between equals, is to let her know she can't control me."

She suggested I refuse to make my bed when I went home for a visit.

My mother went to war with me over it. But she couldn't win the war, because I was doing it for her. It was the only time it was in her face that she couldn't control me. And of course as a child when we went to war, she won all the wars. She is a warrior.

Her rage did not diminish. She went behind my back and in secret and took me out of her will. I never found out till a week after she went to Heaven.

It was a terrible thing she did. More to herself than to me. I guess if I made it crystal clear to her that she can't control me, she made it crystal clear to me, altho I didn't find out till she was in Heaven, that she did not love me.

What an insane way to end. On the next to last day, she relented and arranged that I be given some money. As much as she hated me she didn't want me to be destitute. She just wanted me to have a life of hardship. It's all too crazy for words.

But it all has to be forgiven now. I can't bear the idea that there is any blemish on her happiness in Heaven.

Underneath everything I have always totally passionately loved my mother. I am sure all children do.

You can't not love your mother. That is what you are made of. Loving your mother. It starts with your first breath. And of course there are all the times she was nice to me too. Nice experiences with her.

Yes of course I want my mother to be happy above everything else. I always did. I never would have done the refuse-to-make-my-bed thing if my Higher Self had not convinced me it was for her happiness.

Plus also now I believe after Katy's Higher Self said it on the phone yesterday, that it is causing me problems now, refusing to love my mother now.

For her happiness and my happiness it has to change to pure love and nothing but love. Anything else will interfere with my happiness.

Will obstruct it.

It was very helpful to hear from Katy's Higher Self on the telephone everything about me and my mother and our relationship, loud and clear.

It was everything I knew and experienced but had

always run away from and tried to hide from. Had built all kinds of defenses against facing.

Late in the afternoon I thought about all the changes since I had allowed my Higher Self to get into the act.

Which was soon after we moved to Tucson.

I remembered how afraid I was of my mother, how I saw her as terrifying and awful.

No matter what was going on on the surface, and at that time she was very nice to me, still I didn't trust her and was afraid of her. It came from something under everything.

My Higher Self had worked with me on that by having me give my mother as much love as I possibly could. The love did take away a lot of the fear. Maybe most of it?

But of course what really took away all the fear and all the guilt, was when I came out in the open and didn't let her control me, refused to make my bed, and she went to war with me, and she lost the war.

I didn't fight back of course. It was her war all by herself. I was bystander, on-looker.

After that I went back to pour on the love. I realize now she never accepted any of that love, but of course for me it saved the last 10 years of our relationship while she was in the world.

I wouldn't have been able to bear the idea that my mother without her husband was not receiving a steady stream of love, which is what I was offering her.

And it made me overlook, and almost be unaware of, the steady stream of awfulness she was sending my way.

I just didn't know my mother that well. It didn't occur to me that the steady stream of awfulness was because she was so mad at me and would never stop being mad at me. I just assumed that was what she was like.

Of course she had been lovely to me many times before the refuse-to-make-my-bed incident. But it was when I still had that fear of her under everything.

I would have anxiety when she said she is coming into the city to have lunch with me. And then be relieved when it was over that it had all gone lovely.

My mother really can be lovely, she does have a lovely side. But my experience of it could never penetrate all the way because of the fear underneath.

So when she turned horrid to me those last 10 years, I simply forgot that there had ever been any loveliness.

I assumed that is who she is, a horrid person.

I had no idea it was all for me.

But I can see now it was all stages I had to go thru. I

mean I had to get over that dread of my mother. And what clinched it was her losing her war to control me.

That was what wiped out the whole past. All the fear and guilt of the past were wiped out in one single stroke for both of us.

She never understood what a gift that was to both of us, to wipe the slate clean. All her mother's guilt was gone. All her guilt about all the wars she had won when I was a child. All guilt about everything.

My Higher Self was right, it made the opportunity for a beautiful loving friendship to emerge in its place. That wasn't her choice, but it was what I offered. An authentic relationship of love. That is a great offering.

O well, we have free will, we have free choice. She did not make the choice for her happiness, but that is not my responsibility. Perhaps she will learn from it for her next lifetime. We all learn from our mistakes.

I think her disinheriting me was just a mistake she made. I'm not going to hold it against her anymore. It is time for her to have all love and pure love from me. And nothing else. And just to overlook the big booboo she made at the end.

So thank you Katy's Higher Self. You helped me no end.

I love you.

And thank you Katy. Ours is a miraculous friendship if we can help each other this way.

I love you

Annie

Post script a few days later

Writing this really helped me. To see her disinheriting me as just a booboo she made, turned it into nothing.

Now there was no barrier to love. The instant I finished writing it, I was able to begin having a beautiful loving relationship with her in Heaven.

Katy's Higher Self really did a miraculous favor for me.

March 25th

Anne gets the 3 point turn, Jim is overjoyed

Anne is happy, Jim is pleased

Yesterday evening we went to Mervyns deserted parking
lot to practice the 3 point turn, and this morning Jim drove
us over to DMV (closed on Sundays) to see if I can do it in

the small space you have to do it for their road test.

I had a lovely time being at Mervyns at 5 pm last evening practicing it with Jim. It is our second time of going at 5 pm instead of trying to do it in the morning before my pool opens.

It was luxurious to have all the time we wanted and not have to make it to the pool or lose my swim, pool is only open for lap swim for one hour.

Plus it was a fun change to meet up at 5 pm instead of Jim rolling out of bed and swigging down coffee and rushing over for quickie driving lesson before Anne's swim.

His club is open 24/7 and it is hardship for him that mine is only open that one hour for lap swim.

He calls me when he opens his eyes and asks "do you want to swim today?" and I can tell he always hopes I will say no.

On some rare occasions I do take a whole day off and the boy is overjoyed to hear "you have a day off."

It doesn't happen that frequently, but recently it has been once a week. And I think every morning when he calls when he has just rolled out of bed that is what he hopes to hear.

Yesterday I didn't swim. My Higher Self said "if you

swim you won't want your driving lesson at 5 pm at Mervyns parking lot."

So instead I tried to get my kitchen sink to drain per the instructions on Wikipedia.

I can't believe it is something I tried to do myself, this is the kind of thing Bill always did for me.

But it sounded so easy when I read it on internet.

Heaven only knows what I did wrong, and why it took 4 hours but at last I succeeded.

And got to relax a little in front of TV before I called Jim and said "let's go to Mervyns."

It was lovely. We have been thru hell it seems forever with this durned 3 point turn, it really looked like I would never get it.

But we had big breakthru 4 days ago when we went to Mervyns at 5 pm for first time.

And last evening went swimmingly.

We were both in up mood and made each other laugh a lot in the parking lot, and were both pleased as punch that I was getting it.

And each time I took a break from practicing the 3 point turn, I drove around the empty parking lot so confidently relaxed and excellently, it looked like I was such a good driver. I even teased Jim that he is jealous because I am a better driver than he is.

It was the last thing he ever expected to come out of my mouth that the first time I suggested "he go to jealousy management about it," I laughed so much at how stunned he was to hear that from me.

I think bragging is my favorite thing to do with Jim. I never in my life bragged before. It never crossed my mind to do it. It's not the kind of thing you do with a husband or with a girlfriend

But with Jim I do it all the time. I tell him I am better than he is at knowing football. This kills him, football is his whole life. He has put up with that for a whole year.

And he knows I have never watched a game in my life and don't know how it is played.

But hahaha we bet on who would win Super Bowl and guess who won!

But I didn't rub it in. I had inside information. The morning of Super Bowl while we were driving to DMV, I told Jim "I'll connect in spirit with Tom Brady (the Patriots QB) and ask him."

So I did it all out loud. I asked Tommy if he was going to win this afternoon. He said "No. But I will try my hardest. I will give it my all."

Jim said "you are full of shit."

He thought I was making it up, but it was all real.

So I bet on the Giants. Jim bet on the Patriots.

I barely rubbed it in tho the next day. I was completely restrained. Because it's more fun for me to brag when it is totally ludicrous.

To claim I will teach Jim about football when he actually played for the AZ Wildcats and football is his whole life.

Or to claim he is jealous because I am a better driver than he is. (Jim is the best driver in the world.)

It's always fun to watch him have such a big reaction to that.

But he was so pleased when he drove me home after Mervyns yesterday evening.

His eyes sparkled.

He said "you got A plus."

He glowed.

He really deserved that happiness at my breakthrough in the 3 point turn. He has been thru torture with me for such a long time as I could not get it.

April is amazing

LOL and she climbs another mountain..

April 5th

Of pigeons and Seders

The pigeon watcher..

How interesting that there is a white cloudy mist over our blue sky this morning. The early morning might be chilly anyway till sun rises higher in sky (yesterday afternoon was way too hot).

But this chilly mist makes it a damp chilliness. I am back in my sweatshirt with hood up in front of my open window.

O the boy pigeon is chasing the girl pigeon around the yard. I never knew who was a boy pigeon and who was a girl pigeon until one morning last month while I was lounging in the yard with cup o' coffee and that day's *Letter From God* and I saw some pigeons eating the stale bread I had put out.

But one pigeon was not interested in food. His neck was all puffed up, it looked enormous, and all he did was chase one pigeon who wanted to eat.

He was totally on her tail. And the whole time he was chasing her he was cooing at her.

You don't have to be a detective to figure out what is going on.

So now each time I see a pigeon with his neck all puffed up, enormous like that, not at all interested in food, cooing and chasing another pigeon who seems to want to be left alone, I recognize the mating dance going on right outside my window.

I have been with pigeons my whole life. They all hung out on Riverside Drive (in Manhattan) when I was a little girl brought there to play in the sandbox.

And of course the Lower East Side of Manhattan where I lived for 20 years before I moved to Tucson, is filled with pigeons.

I was surprised to move to Tucson and there were the pigeons here too. And my yard, it appears, is major pigeon hang out.

LOL I have spent my whole life up close and personal with pigeons, but I never recognized a boy pigeon before.

I am becoming more observant about the birds in my backyard. I now recognize the woodpecker's red head and its high spirited call. And the cactus wren's Zorro mask.

I have no idea who does that beautiful singing which has been going on every day and every early evening till sundown.

But it is a great treat. Wherever I am in the house I hear it. Coming from somewhere in my backyard. Maybe high up in the tree which is in the middle of my yard.

If I am watching TV on the bed and mute it during commercials, I hear the song floating in thru my open window. Sometimes I wait before turning sound on TV back on, I want to keep listening till the song is over.

Maybe every Spring all this beautiful clarity of bird song

goes on, but this is the first Spring I have noticed it.

It is not only the bird song which seems more intense and prevalent this Spring, but also the awareness of the holidays.

I began sending out Easter cards on email last week and Passover cards yesterday. It's fun being indiscriminate. Sending both cards to all my friends no matter which religion they are.

I'm sure it didn't do anything for my Jewish friends to get Passover card from me but it totally thrilled Bill's sister, it was her first Passover card.

She was raised Catholic like Bill but became born again on her own as an adult. And she loves her Pastor and her church. And responded to my Passover card by telling me so excitedly her Pastor is having a Seder and they are all invited, and someone is going to explain all about it.

I wonder if this Pesach my sister-in-law is the only one of everyone I know who is going to a Passover Seder.

I myself cannot remember the last one I went to. I have a vague memory of bringing Bill to the family Seder at my aunt Mildred's house.

My father complained to me privately when my uncle Paul went thru all the steps, that his father always said

"Let's get this over with fast and eat!"

But of course for Bill it was his first and only Passover Seder, he was interested in all the steps.

There must have been some discussion at table among all my aunts and uncles and my dad about what it all meant or what was going on in Egypt when this happened.

And it turned out no one knew anything.

Bill said to me privately in the elevator as we were leaving, "It's odd, your family are all intellectuals, but no one has read the Bible."

I guess it is all information which is in the Bible. But my family are all atheists, it never occurred to any of them to read the Bible. Or they would have known something while we were having Passover Seder.

April 6ᵗʰ

LOL My life as an odyssey

If you have a best friend who is in the same boat as you, each of you can help each other, that is when a friend is a true godsend.

For me it was before I found God, but it turned out to be the start of the path back to God for me.

Irene and I were both having catastrophes in our marriage at the same time. It upset us to our bones because we both loved our husbands so much and it was already long term marriage by that time.

Neither of us wanted to give up our marriage when our troubles arose, but everything we were doing was making it worse.

Neither of us could think of what we were doing wrong. It seemed our husbands were doing everything wrong. But we could not stop them or change them, and we were both at the end of our rope.

And suddenly in the middle of a telephone conversation about it, Irene came up with the idea we were doing something wrong. We were not showing mercy. She looked up mercy in the dictionary, and we were not doing that at all.

It turned out to be the solution we were desperate to find. Because we found something we could change in our own understanding and behavior, and not have to change our husband, who we could not succeed in changing.

Both of us were in the middle of a long term war with our husband then.

So first we found mercy, which is what got us out of our anger at them, our grievances with them.

And then we discovered "not fighting back" is the way

to get out of the fighting and how to end the war. Which worked like a charm.

We were able to restore our marriage, our happiness, our peace, and I never fought with my husband again, or with anyone.

I had learned the hard way what fighting does to me. All it does is deplete me and I lose everything.

And after that Irene and I began traveling the path back to God together on the telephone.

She introduced me to Jesus Christ, and I read Rudolph Steiner's book about the Gospel of St John. Irene lent it to me. I didn't absorb anything from it, but it made me open-minded about Jesus Christ.

I think Irene and I were more involved in prayer and with God. We were both involved with God, discovering God. We both became believers at that time.

And of course believing in God for the first time is earth changing, especially after having been atheists our whole life. And because it was all connected up to our marriages, our deepest emotions, and how to relate to our husbands, God was totally real to us. God mattered totally. It was how we had saved our marriages.

Irene found out that there is this thing going on called

the New Age, which is for people like us. That other people just like us were involved in the same thing. It didn't mean we had become a Bible thumper or something which would have been alien to our temperament, join a church.

I think I did try to open up the Bible at first when I discovered God is real. But maybe it was in the middle of Leviticus or something, it was all rules. I could not understand it and it made no sense to me.

And then my first dog, my beloved dog, who I lived and breathed for, became ill. And I heard God talking to me. That is when I entered into conversation with God.

When I first heard Him it was like in the ethers, but I kept listening, and after about an hour it was a voice in my own mind.

I wanted comforting and reassurance so badly that my dog would be all right. God had told me not to take my dog to the doctor, she would be all right, she is healing herself. But my neighbor said "take her to Dr Kuhlman."

I said "Dottie, God said not to."

She said, "Don't listen to God, listen to Dr Kuhlman."

Dottie was a church-goer her whole life, but I don't think she understood about God, not really. Not the God I was discovering, and Who was talking to me all day and all night at that time.

It was just my first 2 days of talking to God all day and all night. It didn't occur to me yet to follow His suggestions implicitly.

So when Dottie said "don't listen to God, listen to Dr Kuhlman," I took my dog to Dr Kuhlman, who did a test, and called me up that evening or the following day and told me it was fatal. She won't live he told me.

I was completely desperate. I was sitting there wondering how I would get thru tomorrow, when I looked up at the TV. It was the evening before Easter and Bill was watching a movie about the life of Christ on the TV.

Jesus was saying "Do not worry about tomorrow, for tomorrow will worry about itself." That instantly helped me so such I wanted to hear more of his words.

Bill had a little pocket Bible on the table where I was sitting. They had given them out on a street corner at CCNY, the college he was going to then.

So I opened it up to the Gospel of St John, because in the book I had read about it by Rudolph Steiner, he said it was the deepest of all the gospels.

And that is what changed my life. It was my first experience of Jesus' actual words. And they went right into my heart and comforted me.

I had still been talking to God all the time, I think it was my 3rd day, altho I probably forgot all about God when I went into that tailspin after Dr Kuhlman's phone call.

Altho I don't know if I did. Because even tho Dr Kuhlman's phone call upset me totally, and I knew I had a serious situation on my hands that I didn't know how to handle.

My first thought was, "OK from now on it is between me and God. The doctors are out of it. I choose to believe God and not Dr Kuhlman."

God of course told me my dog would be fine.

But still I was desperate and upset. Then I heard those comforting words from Jesus in the Easter movie and opened up the Gospel of St John to hear more of his words.

And after I read it thru and received great comfort. Comfort I was desperate for, and so very very very grateful for, I began to hear Jesus talking to me in my own mind.

And so for the next 2 and a half months until my dog did go to Heaven, all I did was read and reread the Gospel of St John and let Jesus talk to me, comfort me, and reassure me, in my own mind.

Till the very last second I did believe my dog would

make it. My belief was that strong by that time, altho appearances were totally against me.

After that I stopped communicating with Jesus or God until ordeals happened in my marriage. I would stay close to Jesus all thru the ordeal to get me thru it.

And 4 years later when it was a huge ordeal and so long lasting, when it was over, I decided to just stay with Jesus in my mind. Never go back to making any decisions on my own, consulting him on everything.

My original experience of Jesus when I first began hearing him in my mind after reading the Gospel of St John thru many times, that first afternoon was an experience of being loved.

I knew I had never been loved in that way before. I had never experienced this kind of love.

In fact I felt like it was my first experience of love, of being loved. I had no idea how wonderful it was to be loved. How much I loved it. How happy it made me, even tho my life was hell because I was so worried about my dog.

I even remember thinking "I am sorry to give up all this love" when my dog went to Heaven and I thought I no longer needed Jesus in my life.

But 4 years later after that huge ordeal, I decided to stay with Jesus even tho now I was having an ordinary life. Life was back to normal. I thought "Why not avail myself of all this help and this love."

And when my next big ordeal rolled around 6 months later and I was tuning into Jesus, to my surprise, a different voice was speaking to me. She was so lovely and so loving.

"Who are you?" I asked.

"I am your mother," she said. "You have a mother. God is your Father and I am your Mother."

And she was so so wonderful to me and I loved her so much. I remember crying, crying tears of joy, at discovering I have a mother. I was so happy to have a mother. There is nothing as wonderful as having a mother.

My relationship with her was different. I was tuned into her all thru my ordeal. And of course I followed all her suggestions to a T.

I let her make all my decisions for me, and I let her love me constantly. That much was the same as with Jesus. But the difference is, she got involved in my thought processes.

I realized I didn't have to think alone, she was thinking with me. I discovered that whatever I thought, was an interpretation of what I was seeing.

And she would interpret it differently. She always interpreted it in a way which did not upset me. Which when I interpreted it, it totally upset me.

I realized every upsetting thought I had was an interpretation, and she would re-interpret it for me which would take away all upset.

That ordeal finally ended, but hot on its heels another one arrived.

And it was during this ordeal that she suggested I move to Tucson. Which I did. A month later we walked into our new Tucson apartment. She worked it all out for me perfectly.

I was still reading Gospel of St John when I arrived in Tucson. I continued to read it all the time. It was my sustenance. But 6 months after we moved to Tucson I discovered *A Course In Miracles* at the public library.

I never went back to the Gospel of St John. I only read that. I fell in love with it from the first page, the *Introduction*. It was just 3 sentences. But I knew the book would take away my fear of the next ordeal occurring.

Moving to Tucson had not been a solution to my ordeals. They occurred in Tucson too. But what Tucson offered me was a fresh new life, with expansion in it, the peace and beauty of nature. Plus I let my Mother set it all up for me.

A Course In Miracles explained who she was. And said the purpose of the *Course* is to bring us into communication with her, and let her direct our lives.

I was already in communication with her, she was already directing my life. The valuable thing *A Course In Miracles* did for me was to prove the past never happened.

It took away the reality of all my past ordeals. I could forget about them, and have a clean slate. It never succeeded in taking away my fear of the next ordeal.

But it meant instantly it was over, there was perfectly clean slate. I believed it never happened. That it was all vivid imagination on my part.

What *A Course In Miracles* did for me was to get rid of all my grievances.

After I finished it I held nothing against anyone ever. I was completely convinced by the *Course* that it never happened, it was all my own vivid imagination.

The author of the *Course* claims he is Jesus Christ and I believe it. It is scribed by a woman in NYC, and she believed it too while she was taking down the words.

To me it makes no difference whether anyone else

believes it or not. I personally do not think the words of love and truth could have come from anyone else.

I truly do believe Jesus was the greatest teacher of God who ever lived. He is my teacher anyway. And I love my teacher and am so grateful to him.

What I realize now, is that someone does not have to hear Jesus in their mind, or Mama (Jesus claims She is the Holy Spirit) to receive all the amazing love I receive from Jesus. Because it's all in the book, even more so.

Someone can receive all that love by reading the book. The experience of reading that book is being loved more than you ever thought possible.

At first I wanted to share the book with everyone. I bought copies for my friends. I told my husband about it. I told all my friends about it.

But after a year of doing this, Mama, who had been so tolerant and patient about all my enthusiasm, pointed out to me this is obnoxious thing to be doing.

I am not helping my friends, I am being obnoxious to them.

"Everyone has their own path back to God, and their path is not my path, and my path is not theirs.

"I would not have liked it if someone pushed their path

on me, and they don't like it that I am pushing my path on them.

"That my friends have all been spectacularly kind and patient putting up with me about all this.

"But enuf is enuf, I have to give them a break. I can love them totally, but that is all I can do. I have to respect their own path, and keep my mouth shut."

Which is good advice and I have heeded it.

I really don't know how my friends put up with me all thru my spiritual path, when I could not shut my mouth, and was pushing it on everyone.

But what could I do! I had discovered something so wonderful, I would not have been human if I didn't want to share it, and for them to have this wonderfulness too.

I guess I am just blessed to have friends and husband who found a way to ignore me. And hope that one day I would go back to being normal friend.

Which thanks to Mama I did. After I finally finished *A Course In Miracles*, which took 3 years to complete.

I used that self control that I finally learned and exercised, "Let anyone believe what they want to believe, they each have their own path," worked in good stead for me when my politics totally changed 10 year later.

When I first made new insights with the help of Mama while I watched the news, she interpreted everything for me, I assumed my husband and my friends would want to hear those insights.

I told my husband and I wrote it in letters to my friends back in NYC. I hadn't made any friends in Tucson yet. I told my friends from NYC on the phone too.

But no one wanted to hear my insights. Bill said "If I wanted to hear about the news, I would turn on the news."

And my friends in New York wanted to see it their way, the way I had always seen it too, not my new way of seeing it.

So I learned to shut my mouth about that too. "Everyone is entitled to their own perception, everyone is entitled to their own political views," Mama kept saying over and over to me.

"You changed your mind all on your own, you would not have liked it if someone pushed you to change your mind."

And so I kept my mouth shut. The critical time was a big election. By now Bill had no idea how much I had changed my views, I had been that good at keeping my mouth shut.

We had always voted the same before but I knew I was

going to vote differently this time.

He kept telling me who he was going to vote for and why, and I kept my mouth shut.

"He can vote for whoever he wants," Mama kept saying.

There was only one point in the car, he was expounding about the primaries before the election or something about the election. He said "of course we hope so-and-so will win."

And I said "There is no *we* about it, I am voting for the other guy."

I actually liked coming out to my husband. I hadn't come out to anyone, none of my friends, none of my relatives. I knew they would be appalled.

After that I went back to keeping my mouth shut with my husband each time he went on and on about the candidate he will vote for.

Altho the men in the locker room at swim pool told him ways his candidate would not be good, and they were voting for the other one. And they were reasons Bill respected. Also his father had come around to seeing things the way I did, and that made a big impact on him too.

I think in the end he voted for the same candidate as me. But what means so much to me is that I had succeeded for the whole year before the election in keeping my mouth shut.

I had not tried in any way to influence his decision making. I had completely respected his free will about it.

I gave myself a big pat on the back for that because I was so passionate about that election. I actually believed the outcome determined whether our country would be saved or not. And at that time all I cared about in the whole world was saving my country.

But it did not sway me from my determination to let my husband have total freedom to think how he wanted and vote how he wanted.

And ditto with everyone else. I kept my mouth shut with everyone.

LOL the country went down the tubes anyway. I will never know if all my monumental effort to save my country paid off in any way. But I followed truth as I saw it and did my best.

April 8th

The 12 egg sponge cake

Breathtakingly beautiful April morning. The world has turned green. All the trees in my backyard are in green leaf.

Our desert sun is so hot and so bright, that one week ago I noticed the new baby leaves were emerging, and now my whole yard is green.

Everything is in full green leaf out there. Altho of course leaves on desert trees do not look like regular leaves, they are tiny green strips which look like they are made out of green lace.

They turn our world green just the same but it means you can always see the blue sky thru the leaves and branches.

There is no such thing as dense green on the desert or bank of leaves. You always see the branches, you always see the blue sky.

As if our trees are all transparent. Nothing here ever blocks out the sky. It is all green lace which branches and sky show thru.

LOL I live in a green lace world now that spring has arrived on the desert, now that our trees are all in full bloom.

And it is the Kelly green of early April, a shade of green I love. As if the green were holding the golden yellow of the sun. A kind of golden green.

A lit up gold in the green shining thru it. As if each leaf holds golden light at its center.

Well this is the week I must show up and take my first road test. Learners permit expires this week and if I don't take my road test before it expires, I will have to take written test all over again.

I am not going to do that! I will show up for road test.

Fortunately all you have to do is show up for road test before Learners Permit expires. If you flunk the road test, there is no deadline for taking it a second and third time.

I don't really expect to pass the road test when I take it for first time this week. All I am asking of myself is that I don't totally embarrass myself. That I do good enuf so I can walk out of there with head held high.

All I want to be able to do is to pat myself on the back for having actually done it.

On my own I would have waited till I was better driver before taking road test, not someone who can barely drive. But I sure do not want to take written test all over again.

Written test is no fun at all, and not that easy to pass. It can be quite tricky and is very suspenseful. Because you are only allowed 6 wrong answers, and you take it on a computer, so each time you answer a question, the computer says whether you got it right or wrong.

And lots of times it says you got it wrong when you were sure you got it right. And sometimes when you guess, it is so suspenseful whether it is right or wrong.

And by the time you have already used up 5 of your 6 allowed wrong answers, you start to pray hard each time you answer a question. There comes a point when you cannot afford even one more wrong answer.

No way do I want to go thru that again. The first time I did not know any of that. And the first time I asked to take the test with pen and paper. And I was sure I had aced it.

The second time I did it on computer. This time I knew I was only allowed 6 wrong answers. And the computer tells you after you answer each question whether you got it wrong or right.

And the second time you don't want to come back for a third time.

All in all it is tremendous motivation for me to take the road test next week, and not have to go back and do that written test all over again.

LOL I will do anything to get out of having to take that written test all over again. Hahaha I never want to take it again.

But of course I am a confident written test taker. I mean I took written tests in school probably from my first spelling test until the day I finally finished college. And never had to take another test again. Until the written test for my drivers license exactly one year ago.

I mean the idea of a written test did not scare me and I approached the first one in a confident and relaxed way. Enjoyed it.

The second one was a different story. I knew I had to pass it or get stuck in a loop of having to keep taking it. You're not free of the written test till you actually pass it.

I have nothing good to say about the written test now. I was enthusiastic about it the first time. I was merry and treated it all as a huge adventure. I was sure I would do so well on it.

But now my attitude about the written test is *I don't want to do it again.*

Which is why I have gone all out to be prepared to take the first road test this week. It doesn't matter whether I pass or fail, just taking it means I never have to take the written test again. Which is all I want.

My attitude toward this first road test is opposite to my attitude toward my first written test.

First of all I had no idea it would be my first written test. I assumed I would pass it. And second of all the only motivation for taking the written test was so I could stop having to read the drivers manual. All I wanted was not to have to look at that drivers manual again.

I thought the instant I take the test I will never have to look at it again. But to my big surprise I flunked the test.

So I came home and read thru it one more time. And went back the next morning to take it again. And this time I passed.

Actually I didn't mind taking the test either time, what I wanted was not to have to read the manual again. Passing the test is the only way to get out of having to read the manual.

I don't really mind written tests, I find them fun. Altho the second one was so suspenseful, one more wrong answer and I flunk.

But I passed and Jim was so proud of me and that was the best part. No one was ever proud of me in my whole life, not that I witnessed anyway.

It is so much fun to see someone beaming and happy and proud of me. It made me feel like I had accomplished a great thing. LOL. It got me all excited. And happy.

Everything is the opposite in my attitude toward taking the road test this week. LOL I have zero confidence. I am sure I am the worst driver to ever be tested on their driving. I see myself as the bottom of the heap.

As far as I can make out everyone in Tucson has been driving since they were 9 years old. They all go in and pass the road test with flying colors. They all score 100. For them it is a piece of cake.

But you know, so what! It's my road test, it's all about me. What difference does it make to me how others do. If they have a great experience and ace it with ease, Mazel Tov! All power to them!

But their life is not my life. It's my life and my road test.

I don't have to be as good as them. I don't even have to be good at it. All I have to do is show up and take it.

And I have worked my ass off to be able to do that 3 point turn which is on the road test.

O my cat Cupcake is chasing a lizard right outside my window. Yesterday it hit 90 degrees and so the lizards came out. I love the lizards, everyone in Tucson does. They are all over our front and back yards.

Well today is Easter Sunday so children everywhere will be hunting for Easter eggs. I didn't know from hunting for Easter eggs till I moved to Tucson and the neighborhood children even looked in my front yard for them.

I grew up in Jewish neighborhood. LOL in a housing project in Jewish neighborhood. Which means we did Trick or Treat in our Halloween costumes like all children everywhere. But Christmas passed by unnoticed. We did not have Christmas trees, we did not have Santa Claus, we did not get Christmas presents.

What we got was a week off from school. We thought that was what Christmas meant. We were thrilled to get a week off from school.

As for Easter it coincided with the Jewish holidays. We got another week off from school for Easter, that is what

Easter meant.

But the Jewish holiday which coincides with Easter, Passover, is a huge deal in a Jewish neighborhood. It means that every family except my family stopped eating bread and ate matzah instead.

When we all opened up our sandwiches in the school cafeteria everyone else had their sandwich on matzah, only I had my sandwich on white bread.

It means that when we were all playing cards at Carol's dinette table, her mother, Ceil, sometimes she would join us in a hand of cards, would spend the whole time talking about her 12 egg sponge cake. And we would all be served a slice of it.

Passover is an 8 day holiday. For 8 days nobody (but me) ate any bread, they ate matzah instead. And you're not allowed to have cake or cookies either. You're only allowed macaroons and sponge cake. My mother is the only one who let us eat cookies and cake all thru Passover. My parents did not follow any of the Jewish rules.

All we did was go to the family Seder at my aunt Mildred's house the first day of Pesach. After that my parents ignored it totally.

Altho since my grandmother came to the family Seder, I

bet every single thing served at table was according to Hoyle. I bet chocolate cake was not served for dessert, just macaroons and sponge cake.

None of her children obeyed any of the rules, but I don't think they broke them in front of her.

She would arrive early to make the matzah balls for the matzah ball soup. And she also made the chopped liver which was served on matzahs, broken pieces of matzahs, as the appetizer.

Then everyone went home and had toast with their eggs next morning. Only my grandmother did all the rules for the whole 8 days.

But the children I played with in my building, Jane and Myrna and Carol, their mothers followed the rules.

At Carol's house her mother got out special set of dishes for Passover. She had 3 sets of dishes. The ones you use when you serve meat at the meal. The ones you use when the meal is dairy. And the ones you use just at Passover. While we were playing cards at the dinette table we saw her take out of the cupboard her special Passover dishes.

Then we heard all about her 12 egg sponge cake as she was putting it up. She only made it at Passover.

I was crazy about cake as a kid, and it always sounded

good to me 12 egg sponge cake. But sponge cake is really a disappointment if you are someone who is crazy about cake.

And ditto with macaroons. You can't get away from macaroons all thru Passover. It is what everyone serves at everyone's house (except for my house). You are always allowed to help yourself to as many macaroons as you like.

And the result is I never had a good attitude about macaroons. I still think of them as what you are allowed to eat when you are not allowed to eat cookies. Which is my same attitude about sponge cake. What you are given when you can't eat cake.

But now that I am in Tucson and not Jewish neighborhood in Flushing, I discover that other children have a ball during Easter. They get to eat as much as candy as they want and they hunt for Easter eggs. For them it is a holiday where dreams come true. Whereas for us it meant we couldn't eat cookies or cake.

I just don't think Jewish holidays are designed with children in mind. They have no concept of what children love.

Whereas for everyone else, they get Christmas and Easter. Which I now discover are dreams come true for children.

But I have no complaint. As kids we didn't know what we were missing out on. And I found it quite pleasant to be sitting at Carol's dinette table with Myrna and Jane and Carol playing cards, while her mother was in the kitchen which was open in front of us clucking about her 12 egg sponge cake.

And sitting down with us and joining us for a hand while the cake was baking. And serving us a slice when it was done.

It may not be the magic of an Easter egg hunt, the thrill of a lifetime which you remember all your life. But it was homey and pleasant. The warm ordinariness of childhood.

April 10

I flunked the road test

Anne flunks!

I flunked in 24 seconds.

Because before you drive with an examiner the lady
takes you out back for you to do your 3 point turn.

She tells you not to knock over any of the orange cones.

Which are all over the area.

When we went on Saturday and Sunday and after 5 pm on weekdays there were no orange cones.

They should leave them up for people to practice, but I guess they think someone will take their orange cones!!!

I guess she told me ahead of time if I hit any one of them I am disqualified.

When Jim and I had gone originally to spy, he saw the orange cones.

But I was too out of it way back then to notice them, or to notice anything. I hadn't even learned how to reverse. I had no idea what I was looking at.

But it turns out Jim had noticed everything, which is why when I kept practicing he told me to complete the turn before I put it in forward.

But I had no idea why he wanted me to do that. To me it seemed more sensible as soon as I backed out to put it in forward for the rest of the turn.

The result is I did it his way in Mervyns lot to please him, but secretly always planned to do it my way during the test.

However he did not know that.

We had gone to Mervyns parking lot an hour before the test, where I did it 3 times his way to make him happy.

So he thought I would ace the test.

However when I tried to do it my way in real life, there was not enuf room to turn around in first gear, the orange cone was right ahead of me.

So I backed up to give myself a little more room.

I didn't know there was an orange cone right behind me.

She said *Disqualified Go home!*

What an anti climax!

It all took place in under a minute.

I had no idea it would be like that. I fully expected to lose points on everything, but I never expected *Disqualified! Go home!*

It was such a let down after all the time energy and concentration I had put into preparing for the test for the 3 weeks before.

I had summoned up every bit of my concentration, my energy, my everything, in preparation for the test, beside all the practicing.

LOL it was a crushing experience to be told *Disqualified Go home* after half a minute.

Plus I had no energy left mentally, emotionally,

physically after it.

It left bitter taste in my mouth, I thought it was mean.

But I am very very glad not to have to think about the test again for quite a while.

I did not enjoy it becoming an obsession and devoting my whole life to preparing for it.

I still have not gotten back my energy mentally, I think it drained me, the intensity of my preparation.

I am sure I will change my attitude about it all and have a better attitude, but right now I think the DMV sucks.

I didn't expect to pass, I thought I would lose too many points to pass, but what happened is not what I expected at all!

April 12

I get email Ryota is coming to visit

I woke up yesterday to email from Ryota. He is my Japanese friend back in NYC. We met in Tompkins Square Park on the Lower East Side when we were both walking our dogs. Both our dogs were puppies then and loved to play with each other.

In the evening we both took our dogs to the playground across the street from the Precinct, since he lived across the street from the Precinct and I lived around the corner.

We would chit chat while our dogs were playing.

Kiki, Ryota's dog, and Clio my dog, were best friends

and loved playing with each other.

If we bumped into each other on the way to Tompkins Square Park in the morning we would take long walk with our dogs instead of letting them play together in the park.

Sometimes we talked and walked around the park together while our dogs played in front of us. Between one thing and another we had a lot of conversation.

Since we moved to Tucson when Clio was 4 years old, all this went on for at least 4 years.

I was closer to Ryota than to any of the other dog walkers because we spent so much time together because of our dogs being best friends. Plus we enjoyed each others company a lot. I found everything he told me interesting.

I guess Ryota is a natural born teacher. I mean he likes telling about things and explaining about things. Everything I know about Japan I learned from him and I learned a lot. And about his life there before he and his wife came to NYC 10 years before.

It is the kind of conversation I like, where everything interests me and I learn a lot from it. I like being told about things. And it is such an enjoyable way, while walking and watching our dogs be in ecstasy playing with each other.

For me it was a totally enjoyable friendship. We were

relaxed with each other. I found it relaxing to be with him. And interesting. Mostly he told me facts, and it turns out facts interest me.

When I mentioned that my neighbor Barry Kessler was married to a Japanese girl, Hiroko. (Barry from the Bronx had met Hiroko in Japan when he was teaching English there.)

Ryota told me that in the days of the Emperor many girls names were off limits to commoners. Only the Emperor was allowed to name his daughters those names. Or the Emperor's family.

And as soon as the reign of the Emperor ended, everyone in Japan named their daughter those names. And Hiroko is one of those names. There are lots and lots of Hirokos now, who are the same age as my neighbor and friend Hiroko.

He told me when you work at a job in Japan and you buy a present for your boss, it has to be a brand name. Only brand names will do. And he named some brand names. They were all American brand names as I remember. I guess expensive ones.

I found out from him that Japan and Korea were always fighting, "just like England and France," he told me. Going way way back thru-out their history.

He said in Japan they all claim that Japan was never invaded, but the dirty little secret is that way way way back in history Korea did invade Japan but no one admits it.

I found out from him that the only food he misses in Japan is that every block has many noodle shops, and there are none here in NYC. He misses the noodles. I don't even know what they are.

He had always wanted to be an artist, and had come from a small town in countryside in the north of Japan to Tokyo as soon as he could. Everyone who wanted to be an artist did.

But in Tokyo all the artists ever talked about was how they wanted to go to New York. That is how I discovered Paris is no longer the art center of the world, now New York City is.

When Ryota came here with his wife 10 years before I met him, he was already an artist. His wife was not. But she told me it was so hard for her to be in a place where she could not speak one word of the language.

She was used to being with her friends all the time and they would talk about movies and stuff that interested them.

Suddenly she had no friends and no one to talk to. And no one to do stuff with or be on the telephone with. She did not even leave the house.

And as a result she began to paint too. And I did go to a show in a neighborhood art gallery of her paintings and his paintings. Ryota did all the work for the show, framing the pictures, hanging them, etc.

I had no idea what her experience had been like till I moved to Tucson. I could speak the language but I had left all my friends behind. It is hard at first.

I guess for Ryota it was easier because he had Japanese painter friends who were here. She had left all her girlfriends behind. I really only had that one conversation with her, when she came to the playground in the evening with Kiki when Ryota was away.

But it was interesting and I learned a lot about her from that conversation.

So I met her once. Ryota never did meet Bill.

I don't know what jobs Ryota had when he first came here, I am guessing working in a Japanese restaurant. When I knew him he was working as a tour guide for a Japanese company, taking Japanese tourists around Manhattan.

It was before cellphones, he had a beeper. Many times I was with him when his beeper beeped.

I guess this meant the Japanese tourists had arrived at Kennedy Airport and he had to go out and meet them.

He told me Japanese like to be told what they are looking at. When he took them thru our neighborhood, he pointed out all the fruit stands and said they all used to be owned by Italians but now they are owned by Koreans.

He is still working at that job all these years later. I bet he is very good at it. Just as everything he told me and explained to me interested me, everything he told the Japanese tourists interested them.

On his dog Kiki's birthday he bought her a whole slice of pizza. Pizza was her favorite thing, and the playground across from the Precinct happened to be next store to a pizzeria. So everyone who hung out at the stone tables and benches there and would want their snack, a lot of times it was pizza.

And when Ryota's back was turned, Kiki would somehow manage to find all the uneaten pizza.

I would notice what she was doing but I wouldn't say anything. But the instant Ryota noticed he took it away from her. I think she bit him a few times when he did that.

That girl loved her pizza.

One year he bought her a Big Mac from McDonalds for her birthday. She loved to eat. He and his wife had adopted their dog from the ASPCA when she was a little puppy.

But he told me my dog Clio was the ideal for Japanese. I can see why, Clio was so slender and elegant and medium sized. She looked the way Japanese look. LOL Kiki was big and klutzy, she did not look Japanese

I think the most fun we had was when we both arrived at same time after a huge snow storm. It was so much fun watching our dogs discovering snow and reveling in it. They rolled and played with each other in the snow.

I think we took a long walk with them in the snow too.

Risqué women on Houston Street where Ryota and I walked our dogs

I missed Ryota very much when we first moved to Tucson. I did write him letters when I got here but I don't remember him responding. Altho every year at Christmas I got a wonderful Christmas card from him, which was always an original artwork by him. It was gorgeous.

After about 12 years, the art work, it was really beautiful, had a photo of his dog Kiki in the middle of it, it was a collage. He said Kiki had gone to Heaven and he wrote "Clio was her first and only friend."

It meant a great deal to me, because for me it was a remembrance of my dog Clio too, and of their friendship. I put a refrigerator magnet on it and still have it up on the side of my refrigerator.

I received his beautiful artwork Christmas cards after that, but I didn't receive one last Christmas. I wondered if he had forgotten me. I did mail him a copy of each of my books when I published them but I never heard from him.

I would write him a long letter after I got each of his Christmas cards and one time I gave him my email address and asked for his.

As soon as I got his email address at Yahoo I was excited, I thought now we will be able to be in touch. But he never responded to any of my emails.

When I published my new novel this past Thanksgiving, I sent it to him, along with my little womens lib book which I had published over the summer.

I found out later that his wife actually read my little womens lib book and liked it because it all took place in their neighborhood 10 years before they arrived. It interested her what my neighborhood was like then.

Because to my joy and surprise I received my first email from Ryota a week after they got the books.

I am amazed he can write email in English. If I were the one living in Japan, I would pick up some of the language as Ryota did here, but I never would be able to write an email in Japanese.

From: Ryoto
To: Anne
Sent: Wednesday, November 30, 2011
Subject: Hi! Anne. I've got books

HI!! Anne and Bill How are you?

First I like to say thank you for beautiful books.

You guys are wonderful, incredibly great couple I ever seen.

We are just fine. We also having wonderful life in

new york.

I'm still drawing some abstract imagination of mine.

And keep working as tour guide. Sometimes busy sometimes slow .

I like this combination. So I can have my own time.

We just came back from Mexico. Only 6 days vacation, but it was wonderful vacation.

We visited Mexico city, Puebla and Cuerunavaca, Pyramids (Teotihuacan).

Landscapes and peoples are beautiful and old city look like somewhere in Europe.

Food was not great but it was ok for us.

Anyway winter has just arrived don't get cold.

Have a nice holiday, I hope see you again. (Hope someday I will visit Tucson to see you.)

Naturally I instantly emailed long letter to him as soon as I finished reading his. I was so happy to hear from him. And very warmed by his warm friendship.

And I never heard from him again on email until I got this one from him this morning. It instantly took me out of my funk about flunking my driving test the day before!

From: Ryoto
Sent: Tuesday, April 10, 2012
Subject: I may be there 4/18 14:00-15:00

Hi !! Anne, Bill how are you?

I'm leaving NY tomorrow for 3 weeks vacation.

Visiting many places including Tucson (off course to see you guys)

Hope you guys schedule to be all right.

I'll call you in morning on 4/18

I'm going to visit pittsburgh, cincinnati, nashville, memphis, new orleans

Houston, san antonio, el paso, tucson, san diego, L.A , san francisco

yosemite, flagstaff, grand canyon, santa Fe, dodge city, wichita, kansas city,

St.louis, Indianapolis, detroit,

3 weeks may not enough to see all.

but it's OK because I never visited central of america and west coast, whole my life.

so now I'm very exciting.

see you soon

Ryota

April 20

My visit with Ryota

I am so happy to see Ryota

It is lush April out there now. The lushness arrived this morning. It is a lush April morning. No longer the delicate thrilling beauty of early April when it is all in bud. Now it is green and lush. It's another world, the warm green lush one. The green is fulfilling itself.

LOL it is rich world, rich and green. A fairyland of greenness, a never never land. The whole world is in its full green leaf. It's a green world with some of summer infusing it. Spring has reached its glory. Although May is still a week away I guess this is what May is.

May is where spring and summer meet, the joining of spring and summer, when spring is totally ripe. That is what I am looking at now. Spring has ripened and is in its full glory. It is an experience like no other.

On Wednesday, 2 afternoons ago, my friend Ryota visited me from New York City. I never went back to visit New York City after I left 20 years ago, the home town where I was born and lived till I moved to Tucson.

Where I was born and grew up and lived my adult life until suddenly out of nowhere I moved to Tucson and began a new life in a new world.

In a place as different from New York City, it could be another planet. And now this new world, this new planet, is my home. And I am happy here. I love my new home, my new place, it is all loveable to me.

"Do you miss New York?" Ryota asked me when we were sitting at the table on my patio looking out at my back yard.

"No" I said.

"At first yes, sometimes," I said, thinking back.

How can you not miss in the beginning all that is familiar to you, all that you have known and ever known, when you are somewhere so far away and different.

You miss the familiar, you miss what is home to you. Because it does take time for a new place to be home.

But now Tucson is home, so it is like having two homes. I never go back to New York City physically, I never want to, but of course it continues to live in my mind.

In my mind I am back and forth between Tucson and New York. How can I not be! Maybe that is what home is, the place where you live, and both abide side by side in my mind and I do go back and forth.

You can't leave home, it is always there. New York continues to live in my mind. It is still as familiar to me as the back of my hand.

And there are ways I will always know it better.

Because Tucson is still a wonder world for me. It is a place of discovery, I am always discovering it. Discovering Tucson, discovering the desert, discovering the people who live here who share my new home with me.

And on Wednesday, two afternoons ago, my best friend

from New York City visited me here. New York City came to me and sat with me and looked out into my yard with me. I got to share Tucson with New York.

It was totally gratifying to have Ryota here. That my life in NYC came to me and sat side by side with me at my patio table, looking out at my yard, even getting a glimpse of my cat. "O a cat!" he said. He spied Priscilla somewhere.

"It is so quiet," is the first thing he said, and I guess it was the truest thing, it is quiet.

Then he looked around. "You have to be a millionaire to have this in New York," he said.

I guess because by New York standards my yard must seem vast, lol as far as the eye can see from New York standards. New York is a teeny weeny world, everything is teeny weeny. Tucson is abundant, everything is abundant. And yes I have an abundant backyard.

He was sitting in quiet looking out at abundance. It was nice to offer this to my friend, a place of quiet and abundance. That he could have it with me for an afternoon.

I had noticed it had gotten very warm an hour before Ryota arrived. I thought "he's not used to heat." Bill's flip flops were still on a little white plastic chair next to front door.

"I will offer them to Ryota to put on for when he sits in my yard" I thought, "because it will be cooler for him if he takes off his shoes and socks."

I thought a Japanese won't find it weird being offered a chance to take off their shoes and sox, and offered flipflops if they want them.

Whenever I watch a movie which takes place in Japan, I see the guest arrive— in the last movie I saw, it was a Jewish lady from Brooklyn. She had met a Japanese man on the boat going over there and he invited her to visit him. And when she arrived at his doorstep I remembered she had to take off her shoes before entering his house.

I would have suggested Ryota just go barefoot. But my experience of men, which means my husband, is he doesn't like going barefoot outside. LOL the desert is filled with sticks and thorns. Bill didn't want to get one.

But after 10 years in our great heat Bill was willing to finally take off his shoes and sox. He did buy a pair of strong sandals to wear all the time and somehow wound up with a pair of flipflops to just walk into the yard. Maybe I bought the flipflops for him, I no longer remember.

Maybe he never wore them, he liked those sandals he bought for himself. But somehow the flipflops wound up on a table in my backyard, and they were on chair in front of the house because I brought them out to offer them to Jim.

Jim is not like my husband, he is Tucson born. Plus different ilk from my husband, he lives in his flipflops. He only wore shoes instead when his flipflops broke some time in November.

To my utter surprise after a gazillion years of living with my husband, when Ryota first arrived and I said at the front door, "Do you want to take off your shoes and socks to be cool, you can wear these."

Instantly he looked glad, had big smile. And then I saw something I never saw in my whole life.

In less than 20 seconds, in less then 10 seconds, in only one second, he got his shoes off, peeled off both his sox and was in the flip flops.

"O they are hot!" he said at first. They had been sitting in the sun.

It took him less time to take off his shoes, peel off his sox, and step into the flip flops than it took my husband to peel off a tee shirt.

Ryota did it standing up and all in one motion. I don't even think I could lift my hands high above my head in the speed which Ryota did to be barefoot in Bill's flipflops

I found it very gratifying that he liked my idea, that he did it, that he was happy with it.

It set the tone for the whole visit, that this was going to be a visit which works. Tucson would meet New York and it would fit like a glove. Everyone was going to be happy. Which is just what happened.

And now to tell about my wonderful visit.

I know how thirsty the desert makes you and it was hot.

I had moved the patio table to the shade of the patio before he arrived when I saw how hot it had become.

It had been in the middle of my yard in the sunshine.

And I put two white plastic chairs by it.

So as soon as he arrived and was in his flip flops I stopped at the refrigerator on the way to outside.

"Do you want something cold to drink?" I asked.

"Yes!" he said.

"I have orange soda" I said. "Or lemonade."

"Lemonade" he said.

I was surprised he did not want a can of ice cold orange soda. I thought it was a better drink. Ice cold and the fizz. But he chose lemonade.

So I filled up a tall glass with ice and brought out the

bottle of lemonade and poured him a glassful at the table.

That must have been when he said "it is so quiet" and "in New York you have to be a millionaire to have this." After that I took him right away to 2 things I wanted him to take a picture of for me.

In the morning when I had moved the patio table to the patio and realized we would be sitting there, I thought those 3 old towels left on the clothesline at the back of the yard would mar the prettiness of the view from the table on the patio. He wouldn't want to look out and see that.

So I went all the way back out there to take them down. And discovered a huge beautiful creosote bush had arrived in my yard and was growing against the back fence. I love creosote with all my heart. I was so grateful it had arrived.

And so I took Ryota back there in his flip flops to see it. I was barefoot of course. I'm not scared of thorns and twigs, I just step lightly.

A cactus tree had grown up in the shade of my huge mesquite tree in middle of yard and Ryota stopped and examined it. He was fascinated.

"It's a tree!" he said. He looked at it carefully. He wasn't interested in my creosote when I showed it to him.

"It has a nice smell" I said, "spicy, instead of flowery."

Then I took him to the side of my house I never go to. Because I had just discovered last week when I was there for some reason I don't remember, that a tree had grown up with orange flowers.

I was thrilled out of my mind. What is as beautiful as orange! It is the greatest blessing I ever got. That, and the creosote bush. I was so thrilled and happy to discover it.

"I'll want you to take a picture of that" I said, "because I never see it."

"How can you never see it?" he asked. Clearly he thought that was impossible.

"My windows don't face it," I simply said. I guess my idea was Ryota would take a photo and I could have it as background on my computer.

He noticed my folded up comforter. I have it folded length-wise next to patio couch in middle of yard. It is where I lounge and watch the birds and drink my coffee in the early morning and read my *Letter from God* for that day. The pillow is there too.

I forgot that Japanese are used to sleeping on futons on the floor. He saw it set up looking like a Japanese futon on the floor and said "Do you sleep here?"

I was so surprised he would recognize that it was a place

I would spend my time lying down, that I would prefer lying on the ground than on the patio couch.

"No" I said, "but I come here at dawn."

Then we went back to my table and we sat down for chat. I refilled his lemonade glass and added more ice.

I asked if he wanted a snack. Jim had called right before Ryota arrived to say "I have taquitos, I can bring them over in less than a minute for your friend."

"Good idea" I said, "yes, thank you, Ryota just called, he will be here in 5 minutes."

And Jim brought them right over with salsa to put on them. "Just heat them in microwave for one minute" he told me.

"Thank you" I said.

I put it by the side of the refrigerator and realized I also have chicken salad to offer Ryota with tomatoes, he might like that.

But when he sat at table and I said "would you like a snack?" he said no thank you, he is full, he just ate.

Ryota told me he drives for 8 hours every day but stops every 2 hours to eat or have a rest stop so I guessed he had eaten 2 hours ago.

I had said in my email to him the day before "I want to

hear all about your trip when you arrive."

I guess he thought I meant "I want to hear how you got the idea to take this trip" because as soon as we returned to table for our iced lemonade —

O I forgot! As soon as Ryota arrived, before he even jumped into his flip flops, when he was getting out of his car, he said "I have a present for you. It is traditional Japanese present." It was wrapped in gold wrapping paper with a translucent gold ribbon. Very pretty.

It was exciting to get a gift. I couldn't remember when I last got one.

"Thank you" I said. I was pleased. "I'll open it in a little while" I said and put it in the middle of the patio table.

I don't think I opened it right away when I returned back from creosote bush (for me) and the cactus tree (for Ryota, that is what he liked most) and tree with orange flowers for me.

I was distracted because I knew now we would have conversation and I was curious what it would be like. LOL we hadn't had a conversation for 20 years and that was while we were walking our dogs.

Now we were sitting at my table to have a conversation. It wasn't the desultory thing going on while he is watching to take the half eaten pizza away from his dog Kiki.

So he said he and his wife, it was last summer and he named a bar on St Marks Place. "You know St Marks Place?" he said.

"How can I not know St Marks Place!" I said drily. But the name of the restaurant or bar I didn't recognize, Ryota thought I would. It wasn't there when I was there but is probably a main place there now. Maybe he caught my blank look when he said the name of the joint which is why he asked if I remember St Marks Place.

St Marks Place is the main drag in the East Village. You can't not know St Marks Place. I moved to the East Village in 1966 and left in 1992, I have probably been up and down St Marks Place one million times. And sat on the stoop there and hung out too in the '60s.

To ask me if I know St Marks Place is to ask me if I know New York.

Ryota was there one summer evening last summer with his wife and someone offered him a free drink. And that is when he got the idea to drive across America.

"Every man," he explained to me, "wants to drive across America. Either on motorcycle" (maybe he didn't know the word for motorcycle, he made with his hands driving a motorcycle) "or a car.

"Every man wants to do this," he explained to me. Or maybe he was telling me what he explained to his wife.

"Every man wants to do this," he explained to his wife at the time and to me in Tucson now. "And I am a man. I want to do this."

But the idea didn't take hold till October. That is when he got out all the maps. And began to study them. That is when the plan was made. He studied all the maps for 6 months and planned out his trip.

Then he got out the little book where he had written down every tour he had made for the Japanese tourist agency he works for, going back 30 years since he first began working for them.

Taking the Japanese tourists around New York City. Apparently he gets paid for each tour he does. He doesn't get a regular salary, just paid for each tour.

And he discovered for 30 years April has the least. He had hardly worked in April. So he decided he would make his trip in April.

Meanwhile it seems when Ryota is not working he hangs around the house. Apartments in the East Village, the tenement apartment Bill and I used to live in and where

Ryota and his wife Taeko still live, are tiny.

As I told Jim the other day they're same size as the apartment *The Honeymooners* lived in, Ralph and Alice's apartment.

Ryota had emailed me back in November that he is still working for that Japanese tourist company and when he is not working he is home doing his art. "So it is perfect."

But apparently it is driving his wife nuts that he is always home except when he is working.

"Can't you have a hobby," she said. "Can't you go fishing. Can't you get friends and go out with your friends. You need a hobby," she said.

"Why do I have to have a hobby," he said. "I am an artist. Artists don't have to have hobbies."

So anyway when he explained to her how he wants to take this trip driving all around America, and all men want to do it, and he is a man. She said she won't go. She gets carsick after 3 days. And the trip is for 3 weeks.

"Are you sure?" he said when she said about getting carsick. "Isn't there something you can do?"

"No" she said, "there's nothing I can do."

"You go by yourself," she said.

At first he didn't know what to do, he wanted his wife

with him.

But I was laughing at this point. It was so clear to me his wife just wanted him out of the house. She really really wanted him to go on this trip for 3 weeks.

She had no luck trying to talk him into getting a hobby like going fishing. For her his trip was answer to a prayer. 3 whole weeks of the house to herself.

Taeko had become a painter herself when she arrived in NYC, could not speak a word of English, could not go out because she could not talk the language, did not have her friends here, knew no one.

Her husband was a painter and he set her up and helped her get started. And now I secretly think she is more passionate about her art than Ryota is. Because he told me on my patio, "she is like you, the way you are about your writing she is about her art."

Also I think her art is the same as my writing. Because Ryota told me the way it is unconventional, he described it to me, I think Taeko is doing in her painting what I do in my writing. I think Ryota might even realize that.

In any case even tho Taeko now has lots of friends (Ryota told me "lots and lots of friends, both Japanese and American") what she really lives for is her art, that is what she cares about.

I became a writer in the East Village, Bill is the one who got me to do it. And I guess it is the same for Taeko. It was not Ryota's idea she become an artist, but he took her from Tokyo to New York, she had no choice. It was the solution she found for herself when she had no life and could not leave the house at first.

I guess Taeko now has my life in New York (the life I had when I lived there). Lots and lots of friends and living and breathing for her art. Doing it all the time.

That is probably half the reason she wants Ryota out of her hair. When she is not seeing her friends she wants to be left alone to do her art.

I also found out from Ryota that the books I wrote which I sent him, he didn't read but his wife did. She likes them. And the drawing Bill did of the woman when he first started art school, a drawing I love and which I had Bill frame for me and put up on my bedroom wall, I had put that in my last book. And Taeko loves it, she says it looks just like her.

Ryota of course is a little dismayed his wife wants him to have a hobby and was so happy he was going to take this trip alone. When he wavered when he found out she would not go, she really encouraged him to do it.

"That is great" I said to Ryota, "you have a wife who wants you to have freedom. What can be better! You have a wife you really like, you find her interesting, you really like Taeko, and freedom at the same time. Perfect!"

It wasn't exactly how he saw it. His feelings had been a little hurt when she kept saying he has to have a hobby. Like going fishing.

She came up with a great idea. To live in the East Village and have fishing be your hobby, meant he would be gone for at least 24 hours each time he went fishing.

Oddly enuf fishing was my husband's hobby when we lived in the East Village. I know all about fishing trips.

Bill never liked sitting around the house when he wasn't working. He always had a hobby. First fishing. Then playing hand ball. Then bouldering in Central Park.

Bouldering is rock climbing, but instead of climbing up the rocks, you dance around the rock. And you don't need equipment, just climbing shoes. You dance with the rock.

The best boulderer of all was Japanese. Yuki. Bill loved Yuki. Yuki was his best friend. Bill and I had that in common the 4 years before we left NYC.

He would go to Central Park to boulder and there he

would see Yuki. And I would walk my dog Clio and bump into Ryota. Each of us wound up for our own best friend those last days was Japanese.

Yuki was probably an artist too. All the Japanese who came here came here for their art. But Yuki had a hobby too, bouldering. And he was magnificent at it according to Bill.

I heard a lot about Yuki, what he likes to eat, what he likes to do, where he works, I guess in a Japanese restaurant, and especially about Yuki's bouldering. He was Bill's ideal.

First Ryota went to Pittsburgh. He didn't have much to say about the town. It took him 8 hours to get there. And then he could not find a hotel. He went to 10 hotels, they were all full. Finally he gave up and slept in his car.

Then the ride to Memphis was thru Appalachia. "One hour sunny blue sky, one hour rain, one hour sunny blue sky, one hour rain. But the rain is different. It is white."

In Memphis he went to the street which is all music. Either they sell the music instruments or it is bars and clubs playing music. I forget the name of the street he told me.

"Memphis" he said, "you know, Elvis Presley." The street is not that long, Ryota told me how many blocks.

Ryota loved it. He likes Memphis.

Then he went to New Orleans. To Bourbon Street. Which again is all music and bars and clubs and restaurants. O Ryota loved Bourbon Street. It was his favorite thing in the whole world.

He loves New Orleans. He told me he does not like just white, he likes everything, and New Orleans had it. Spanish, French, black, white. He loved it. And the food was delicious. "So sophisticated" he told me.

Then he went to the French Quarter which he said is just like Brooklyn Heights. Who knew?

I always assumed the French Quarter would be more colorful, a little more down and out. Brooklyn Heights is totally hotsy totsy now. And is a quiet residential neighborhood. I always pictured the French Quarter of New Orleans as hopping!

Jim just arrived to take me swimming. To be continued.
I'll write the second half of the story tomorrow.
This is Bill's drawing Taeko liked so much.
Ryota said, "she says it is her."

"Taeko says it is her"

April 22

Part 2 of Ryota's visit

It is beautiful. There is nothing quite like it. This garden of eden morning. The sensuality of summer has entered the spring. Spring culminates, reaches its height, when the sensuality of summer enters it turning the world lush.

There is no beauty like it. None greater. It is what dreams are made of. The point where spring and summer join. It is what happiness looks like. It is what poets write poems to and children sing and dance about.

Perhaps it is what has inspired music and art, brought them into being, called them forth, because it is irresistible.

No matter where you are or who you are, it calls something forth in you. LOL it is an Easter basket and May Day all wrapped up in one.

The Easter bunny with his Easter basket, hippity hop.

And "here we go picking nuts in May," children dancing around a May Pole. It is where April meets May, and more than that there not is.

O my Ryota where are you now on your travels. It is the middle of second week of your trip, the exact middle of your trip. You are on the road somewhere, but where to? and where from?

Have you reached San Francisco yet? Are you enjoying that city. Is it made for you? The influence of the Orient is very great there, it has such a Japanese feel. San Francisco where New York meets Japan.

And you're back up north now, you have left the south. Are you happy to be back up north? What you are used to. Or have you gotten addicted to the south and the southwest in this one short week.

San Francisco where Japan meets New York City, is it your cup of tea? It is probably what your mind looks like, your whole life rolled up into one. It must look familiar to you, this place where Japan and New York City meet.

You, who grew up in Japan, and spent your adult life in New York City and never left till you found yourself driving along our beautiful southwestern desert last week.

The cowboy movies you watched as a kid in Japan

suddenly sprawling in front of you, the world of desert and cactus and sky. And desert mountains which you said "are so unusual, such unusual shapes."

LOL you walked out of the movies of your boyhood into the real thing. Shall I buy you a cowboy hat Ryota. Do you want spurs. How about cap pistol?

Did you know you were going to arrive at the place where the movies were made, where all the movies took place. You wanted to drive around America and you did and you are.

You drove to Pittsburgh, and then thru the Appalachias to Memphis. Then on to New Orleans and over to Houston.

And then to San Antonio and El Paso and then to me in Tucson.

And then to San Diego and up the coast to L.A. And then all the way up the coast, and right now you are arriving in San Francisco, probably you'll arrive there tonight.

Are you still driving along the Pacific Ocean? The ocean which cradled you, which was your whole life, till you moved to New York City and lived on the Atlantic Ocean instead.

O city boy, ocean boy, is San Francisco your city. You

who have lived and loved New York City for 34 years, who dreamed only of it while you still lived in Tokyo, wanting only New York.

You who left your parents' home in the countryside of northern Japan to come to Tokyo.

You came at 17, the age we all leave home to go to the big city. Which we all did. Your big city was Tokyo. I moved from Flushing to Manhattan.

You spent the '60s in Tokyo with artists and the revolutionaries. You too were an artist and revolutionary.

I wasn't an artist then, just a revolutionary. I didn't know from art, I only knew from revolution. You didn't know from revolution, you only knew from art. And yet we had the same Sixties, you in Tokyo, me in New York.

And as soon as the bloom was off the rose of the Sixties you had your new dream, your new exciting dream. You and your fellow artists, you dreamt only of coming to New York City.

In Tokyo you met your wife. She wasn't an artist, she was like me, an intellectual. She talked about movies and books with her friends. Like me she was a revolutionary and a hippie.

Your wonderful wild adventurous wife. And then in

1977 you made the great adventure happen. You both arrived in New York City.

And never left till you set off to see America 10 days ago. It still blows my mind that you drove thru 2 days of Texas desert before you arrived in my front yard and sat in my backyard with me.

And stood in my kitchen to show me how to sharpen the knife.

I knew you would know how to do that. My husband had such a Japanese side. I would always come across him meditatively sharpening the knife on that stone block.

And when I saw that the knife had become dull, was having a hard time cutting me a slice of bread, and I knew you were coming, I put the knife and stone block together right by the frig, so I could ask you to sharpen the knife for me.

I was too shy to say "can you sharpen it for me." Instead I said "can you show me how to sharpen it." I hadn't realized what a long job it was. You, who love to teach, gladly showed me how. You didn't finish the job. "It still needs a lot of work" you said, "you have to do it every week."

There was too much going on in my mind to actually

pay attention to what you did and how you did it. I hadn't expected to learn how to do it, I had just thought you would do it for me. But you gave me instruction and I watched you do some of it. Who knows maybe I will try to do what I thought I saw you do.

And that was the end of the visit. After that we went back to my front yard for pictures.

I had forgotten all about that I had asked you in the beginning how to sharpen my knife but you remembered.

When you said it is time for you to go, "let's do the knife now," and stood over the sink to sharpen it with water running on the stone block.

You showed me how the block has to be wet and to keep it wet. "Let the water drip on it all thru it."

I wonder if my husband knew that. Did he always do it over the sink? Is that why the stone block to sharpen the knife is on top of the sink.

And then we took a few photos in my front yard and you were off. You had me take a photo of you in front of my house so you could show your wife.

You showed me how to work the camera. You didn't like the first photo I took. "Why, did I do something wrong?"

"No" you said, "I just look funny in it. Do another."

I guess with these new cameras you can see right away what the photo looks like, and you didn't like how you looked.

The second time I did do something wrong, the picture wasn't there. "You forgot to press the button" and then we did a third,

And this one you must have been satisfied with because we didn't do another.

Then you got out a tablet and took a photo of my house with that, I guess to show your wife.

And then I had you walk to the corner of my yard and take a pic of the fire plug I had crashed into when I was first learning how to reverse last month. I want to show it to Jim and tease him about it.

After Ryota finished telling me about New Orleans, he really liked New Orleans, he said Tucson is boring.

"Yes" I said "Tucson is boring."

"Not Tucson!" he said, "Houston!"

"O Houston!" I said.

"Yes Houston," he said. (I am happy it is Houston not Tucson he says is boring. I love Tucson but it is not New York or New Orleans.)

Ryota said "Houston is boring." He went to downtown Houston of course. Downtown is always the interesting part of any town. But he said the map showed it as downtown but it doesn't look like a downtown of a city.

"It looks like midtown in New York," he told me, "just big office buildings and no one on the street."

Then he went to San Antonio and to my big surprise he loved San Antonio. He tried to tell me the Alamo is there. "They come, many Texas tourists, because of the Alamo."

But how can I understand Ryota's accent! He told me his English has not improved one bit since I left New York because so many Japanese moved to New York, so many moved to our neighborhood.

"On your block and my old block, on 5th Street and 4th Street, every building has 4 or 5 Japanese living in it. The landlords like to rent to Japanese because they always pay their rent," Ryota explained.

So Ryota is friends with all the Japanese who have moved into the neighborhood. And his job is a tour guide for a Japanese company showing Japanese tourists around New York.

If his friends in New York now are all Japanese, and he speaks Japanese with his wife, and his job is all speaking

Japanese. No wonder his English has not improved in the 20 years since I left.

Usually I understand what he is saying because I can guess the word from the context.

But how in the world would I ever guess he is saying Alamo to me. Never in my whole life did I think the word Alamo would come out of his mouth.

It's barely in my consciousness and I grew up watching Davy Crockett. All the kids in my grade school did back then. It was a Walt Disney show and it was a huge deal, and we all sang the song together in class. *Davy, Davy Crockett, King of the wild frontier.*

It was a mini series which ended at the Alamo. That was not my favorite part, my favorite parts were when he was living in the woods.

But it ended at the Alamo. Somehow I knew a big fight like a war or battle took place at the Alamo, whatever that was, maybe a fort. And that was the end of Davy Crockett.

And then maybe some time later I picked up it had been a fight between Mexico and Texas, a war, and I guess I knew Texas won the war at the end because it became Texas and not Mexico, they freed themselves from Mexico.

That was what Ryota explained to me too. He said all

the Texans come there, all the Texas tourists, because of the Alamo.

It took 6 tries before I realized he was saying Alamo and then he went on, "it was for freedom and independence, they got their freedom."

I had no idea the Alamo was in San Antonio. I had no idea where the Alamo was, just that it is in Texas.

And then he said a river runs thru it and the river is very low now. He showed me how low. I gather the river runs right thru the middle of the city.

Ryota loved it and I did too. I would love to live in city where a river runs right down the middle of it. I love rivers. Secretly I have zero desire to see the Alamo but I sure would like to see the river running thru San Antonio.

He really likes San Antonio. I can't describe it. The two cities he liked before it were Memphis and New Orleans.

He liked Memphis because of the long street, altho it didn't sound that long when Ryota told me exactly how long it is. But it is where all the music takes place, all the clubs and bars and studios and music stores. It is all about music. It is where music happens. Ryota really liked it, it was just what he was looking for in Memphis.

And New Orleans of course had everything he was

looking for. He loved New Orleans because of Bourbon Street. It's everything he loves in one package. The people, the food, the music, the color, the life, everything! New Orleans was made for him and he liked the French Quarter very much too.

After that I guess Houston was a big let down. Even tho they called it downtown, it was just huge office buildings and no one on the street.

But what surprised me so much (and I think surprised him) is he fell in love with San Antonio.

It didn't seem to have anything he was looking for in the other cities. If it had a downtown he didn't mention it. All he talked about was the river and the Alamo. Is it possible Ryota loved the Alamo? He sure did like the river thru the middle of the city.

His falling in love with San Antonio is not one bit like his loving New Orleans so much. With New Orleans he said all the wonderful things it has. People of all colors and races, French and Spanish, black and white, Indian. "I don't just like white" he told me.

And the food is so sophisticated.

And the music he loved.

He loved it all.

San Antonio was completely different. He just looked happy when he told me about San Antonio. Other than the river and the Alamo he didn't say anything else except "It was good."

"San Antonio is good," he said. He said it 4 different times, four different ways. "San Antonio is good." Thinking about San Antonio made him happy. He just sat there happily with happy smile on his face saying "San Antonio is good."

"You love San Antonio!" I said. It dawned on me. "You love it, you love San Antonio."

"Yes" he said, "I love it."

My mind was blown. Ryota had found the city he loves. And it was not for any reason that he loves cities.

"You love San Antonio" I said again.

"It is nice" he said. That was another thing he said several times with the same purring happiness about it. "It is nice."

"You must have been a Texan in your past life Ryota, you love Texas, you love San Antonio. San Antonio is what you love."

"Yes I love it," he said again. "It is nice."

And I do think Ryota was Texan in his past life. I think

he felt good there.

He fell in love with the desert too. He said he drove thru it for 2 days before he got to Tucson. I was thrilled he fell in love with the desert, that I could share this love with him.

We only got to talk about Japan one time in our conversation at my table on my patio in backyard.

He didn't like El Paso, that was the city he was in before he came to Tucson. I told Jim and Jim said "Who does! El Paso is awful. The wind blows dust on you all the time. There is nothing good about El Paso."

Ryota didn't say what he didn't like about El Paso, I think he just made a face.

I got the impression it is very close to Mexico, you can walk across. But maybe I am wrong. I don't know the cities in Texas.

"Because" he said, "El Paso has two churches which were built long time ago, like 1600s," so Ryota went to visit one the morning he left for Tucson.

"So you went to church this morning!" I exclaimed giggling.

He was taken aback. "I don't believe in anything," he said to me right away. He can't tell when I am teasing, he doesn't know my humor.

"I don't believe in anything," he said to me.

"What is Japan" I asked, "is it Buddhist?"

He said how he doesn't believe in anything but in Japan "you grow up in it, it is your family, it is all around you, it is everyone, it is everywhere. It doesn't mean you believe in it."

"I understand" I said, "it was same for me living in a Jewish neighborhood. I didn't believe in any of it either, but it was still my life."

"Is Japan Buddhist or" (I tried to think of another religion it could be. The word Shinto came into my mind) "or Shinto?"

He said "Shinto is like what the Romans were before Christ. It is very old, it goes way back."

"O I know, like nature religion, they worship nature."

"Yes" he said. "But then in the year 700 Buddhism came."

"It came from India? Right?" I said.

"We imported it from China," he said.

"O" I said. "It came from India, then to China, and then you imported it from China."

"Yes" he said.

"And then the Governor said we all had to be Buddhist."

After that it seemed like they went back and forth. One Governor said everyone in Japan had to be Buddhist, so they were all Buddhist. Then another one said they could be both, Buddhist and Shinto, so they had both religions.

And so Ryota said, "In Japan when you get married, the marriage party, the celebration, is Shinto. But when you die it is Buddhist."

When he said "when you die it is Buddhist," I burst out laughing and laughed for 10 minutes. I could not stop laughing.

The first thought which went thru my head was "the Japanese are nuts." But it didn't seem polite to say that. Instead I said "the Japanese are so creative, they are so sensible."

But I couldn't help myself. "When they marry it's Shinto, when they die it is Buddhist," I couldn't stop cracking up.

And even tho I said "they are so creative and so sensible," either he read my mind when my first thought was "the Japanese are nuts," or what hit me, hit him at the same time.

"The Japanese are crazy," he said to me.

"No" I said, "they are so creative."

I laughed so hard because I thought they are nuts.

But also, and I said it 3 times in between whoops of laughter, and each time I said it, it set off more gales of laughter, "When they die they are Buddhist."

I think it is because of the word die too. Ever since Bill went to Heaven this time last year that word has never come out of my lips and I won't let anyone say it to my face either.

After all my entire happiness depends on believing he never died, no one does, he is alive and well and happy in Heaven.

I even believe now that death itself is all just an imagination. We are always in Heaven, we never left, and death is just a strange dream which takes place in imagination not in real life.

But because my entire happiness depends upon believing this. And because there is zero reinforcement from the world in believing this, the whole world except me believes death is real, I try to be vigilant in protecting my belief.

God forbid I lose my belief in this, I would lose all my

happiness. I don't even want to think about it. My life would be tragedy instead of joy if I thought for an instant anything bad happened to my beloved husband.

Obviously if my belief were solid as a rock I wouldn't have to be careful of what I say, or what I think, or what I let others say to my face. Maybe trying to believe it, or wanting to believe it, is more accurate.

I'm not there yet but it is where I want to be. And I have summoned up everything I have to be there. But obviously I have not accomplished it yet if I won't let anyone say die, died, death to my face.

Which is another reason I cracked up when Ryota said "but when they die, it is Buddhist." It was the word die which struck my funnybone so much too.

I kept repeating "when they die they are Buddhist" and each time I said it I cracked up all over again. In fact I never stopped laughing. I would say it again amidst gales of laughter and laugh even harder.

It even crossed my mind when I finally settled down again, "Well Anne you're laughing at death. Has that what it has come down to! You find it so funny."

I guess after having been so afraid of the word for one solid year, 24/7 for one solid year, the bogey man was over,

I now just found it all such a riot.

So you see it was the combination which set me off, my first thought that the Japanese are crazy, and that the word die was so funny.

I have no idea what Ryota thought when he saw me burst out laughing for 10 solid minutes at something he had just said.

I just laughed and laughed and laughed with joy and delight. It rang out all over my yard.

And I guess that was the high point of the visit for me. It just erased any distance between him and me. He was no longer my friend from New York, he was no longer visiting me in Tucson.

We were just being together. We were being. He was totally in my world. Not the Tucson world. But the world of my mind and heart. The world I really live in.

And then he went to get his camera from the car. And he took the photos I wanted of Bill's 3 paintings and I got out Bill's tapestries and held them up so he could photo them too.

And then I put more ice in his lemonade. And he said "Time to go. Let me show you how to do the knife." And he stood over my sink and showed me how to do the knife.

And then we did the front yard photos, the pic of him for his wife, and he took the pic of my fireplug for me.

And we shook hands and we both said what a nice time we had.

And he said "Which is the way to I 10" and I said "I don't know. It's in that direction."

It's in that direction

He's back home, he loved his trip..

Easy Rider returns home

From: Ryota
To: Anne
Sent: Wednesday, May 02
Subject: Hi! Anne. How are you?

Dear Anne.

Well, so I came back to new york yesterday.

This trip was so wonderful, so succeeded

especially Texas, Arizona, Yosemite, Sedona, Grand

Canyon, Monumental Valley, Mesa Verde and Santa Fe.

So beautiful, and drive a car so free, no traffic jam

75 miles per hour.

Every things are So big. America is so big.

Anyway it took 21 days and I feel very happy about it.

Now I send pictures of Bills works and some other
things. Those pictures came out very good.

So hope see you soon.

Ryota

From: Ryota
Sent: Thursday, May 03
Subject: Hi!! Anne

I'm happy with that you are happy with my job on
your photos.

It came out really great.

And I saw that movie last year some where in new
york

maybe internet, I've forgot it. But I remember whole
story.

That was real good movie. I think.

I liked St. Antonio and St. Diego and all desert which
I have pass through 80 miles per hour.

That made me feel like a easy rider (remember that
movie).

It was great experience. Also I saw double rainbow.

Have you ever seen that?

Anyway I'll send a photo to you.

From: Ryota
Sent: Monday, May 07, 2012

Hi ! Anne I've been so great since I came back to new york.

How are you?

I like west coast and central of america and east coast. I like all america.

But when I got into manhattan I realized that new york is so big so safe so many people.

And new york is free, especially east village. no place like this in america. we only miss nature things

But you have both of them right? now you got freedom and nature. having good life.

Taeko seems happy with my trip, and now she started think about going to travel with me by car.

She likes traveling only trouble is carsick.

And one of my old friend who lives in japan also interested in second trip, may be next time will be Canada, Yellow stone or Florida , etc.

He came new york 3 times already but never been
other places in USA. He will retire next year so He
will be 100% free. Hope we can make within 2,3 years.
Well this is only plan so far.
So any way Anne, keep that way, enjoy your life.
I LOVE YOU.

Thank you dear Ryota for the wonderful visit
Thank you for fixing my knife it cuts exquisitely now

Remember you always have a friend in Tucson

April 21

My darling generation

A lovely dawn is still happening. It is restful to the eye. That it is first light. Color is so muted, and the air is so cool.

Ryota said when he arrived in New York it was the time of punk rock. It was going on in our neighborhood and he and his wife went to see all the bands.

He said "You know what punk is, you don't have to be able to play an instrument, anyone can stand up there and do it."

He was very excited about it, his eyes glittered when he told me about punk rock, his body became excited.

I guess it was a big thing to just arrive from Tokyo right at the start of punk rock in all those seedy clubs on the Bowery. Seedy clubs on a seedy street. With all that huge excitement happening inside them.

It was still a down and out neighborhood back when I left New York. We all lived there for the cheap rent, plus it was relaxing to be there. It was made up of the immigrants who had never bettered themselves.

Their brothers and sisters had all bettered themselves and moved to nice houses on Long Island or in Brooklyn or Staten Island.

These are the ones who had not, were still living in the tenement apartment where they were born. They did not have drive or ambition.

They were content simply to be. To go right on having the same life they had always had, and shop at the same little stores where the owners knew them since they were a little girl. They never left home.

They were my neighbors and I loved them. And they were everyone's neighbors in every building back then. They are what turned our neighborhood into family.

It was like having aunts and uncles and cousins and grandparents who were totally accepting (unlike our own parents and relatives who expected us to succeed, and were so upset that we weren't, that we had chosen to drop out instead).

They thought we were just fine. The way we were seemed natural to them. It didn't seem unusual to them we had chosen to live in tenement walk-ups in a poor neighborhood. It is where they lived and they were happy here.

For them it seemed natural to live here, and they found us living here natural. And they liked us, and we liked them. The Lower East Side back then was a warm nest.

It is really why we all stayed there forever and didn't leave till we were pushed out.

No one expects to find themselves in a warm loving nest when they are all grown up, and it was never what we were looking for.

We didn't leave home to find ourselves in a place where our parents only went back to visit their mothers.

All the mothers of the immigrants who had succeeded still lived there. In the apartments where the successful immigrants had grown up.

We had moved to the East Village originally back in the Sixties because it was so cool. When the Sixties first arrived in New York it started in the East Village.

As Bill's friend Max once said "we were refugees from the middle class."

We didn't want to be middle class. We were intellectuals, we were idealists, and above everything else we were adventurers. We wanted adventure. And we were hippies. And we were revolutionaries.

The rent back then was $50 a month, we could afford to live there and have our own apartment.

I wasn't in an artist world when I first came there in the '60s, but I think young artists from all over the country came there too.

It is where the Sixties generation lived when they lived in New York. We were the Sixties in New York City. We were the hippie neighborhood.

When we turned 30, most of us wanted to leave the city and move to the countryside. And I think most did. I was among those who wanted to, but couldn't figure out how to do it.

I was longing for the peace and beauty of nature now. I had had enough city. I was ready for the party to be over, I was partied out.

Then the generation just behind us arrived. As a girl from L.A. explained to me— (She had just arrived from L.A. and was walking her dog in the park. She had been trying to break into being a screen writer in Hollywood. I guess she was still a screen writer. She was an LA girl.)

She said to me "Your generation has no ambition, they just want to drop out. But we have ambition, we are striving, we want the jobs. But we can't get them because your generation got them and won't leave.

"Your generation likes pot because you want to sleep. We like coke because it makes us work harder."

(It wasn't how we thought about pot, as my friend Michael said, "you lie on your bed and smoke a joint and all the wisdom of the Universe pours down on you.")

She arrived at same time punk rock started, and they were the new punk generation I guess. Some of the punks walked their dogs in the park too and their dogs had punk names. They named their dog Rocket instead of Dandelion.

I liked the punks when they first arrived. I was fascinated by their bad taste. We were brought up to dress in good taste. We were third generation immigrant, dressing in good taste was a big deal to us. We were brought up to believe good taste matters.

What we loved about the Sixties was dropping out of all that. What we loved about the Sixties was the freedom.

It was like being a child again because you could wear whatever you want instead of how you are supposed to dress.

I went back to my little girl taste. I liked pretty, I liked sparkles. I liked beautiful bright colors (not beige!). Crimsons and emerald green and turquoise, and purples. And sequins and satin and velvet.

The Indians had opened up inexpensive clothing stores all over the East Village with just the kind of clothes I liked. It turned out I like Indian clothes.

The tops all had halter backs. It was the kind of clothes I really like, pretty, and feminine and fun. And sexy too.

I had been brought up that the ideal was to dress like British aristocracy. It is the world of suits, and cashmere sweaters and pleated skirts.

Understated, that is the word, or the ideal. Everything be understated and in very good taste. Beige was big!

Indian clothes have tiny little mirrors sewn all over it. And sparkles. It is what I like. And you can wear little bells tied around your ankles which tinkle when you walk.

The Sixties was all about play. You drop out of society and just play. Drop out of convention and just play.

Junior high school is what turned us into convention. That is when we went all out to fit in. And junior high school never ended until the Sixties came along and liberated us from it.

The boys let their hair grow long and wore headbands. If we all dressed like Indian princesses from India, the boys all dressed like Apaches.

We looked like we had just arrived from India, they looked like they had just moved off the reservation.

And then we all smoked pot and got stoned together and had lots of fun. And danced in Tompkins Square Park to the Sixties bands who were arriving from California. Everything was free and outside and fun.

And play.

I really can't speak for another generation because I'm not it and don't know it from the inside. I can only speak to my own generation and we were all about freedom.

I know that Los Angeles screen writer who had just arrived in New York looked down on my generation. She believed in her own, the one right behind us.

Our generation was looked down on by everyone, the

one just ahead of us, the one just behind us.

When Cora applied for a secretary job, she said "I gave them your phone number, Anne." She didn't have a phone then.

And when the guy called I guess he had a lot of time on his hands. This was 1969, by then everyone had heard of the Sixties. And he said all the great things about his generation, and how "your generation just wants to contemplate their navels."

I didn't say anything. I was so young and sweet, I was just so pleased that a grown up wanted to talk to me. A boss, an employer.

I was just so surprised he had so many bad things to say about my generation. I had never even thought of being in a generation. We were all kids, that is what kids did then.

I guess I thought the Sixties was an amazing thing. I remembered how life had been before it. And it was a great liberation. I loved it. I never went back.

And I guess that was the thing about the East Village. Maybe when nearly all the hippies moved out, maybe they didn't all move to the country side, maybe they did move to nicer neighborhoods. They stopped being drop outs.

Those of us who stayed never went back into society.

We stayed dropped out. We liked being dropped out.

My parents were hysterical of course. All my cousins went to graduate school and became professionals. Which is what I was supposed to do too.

And I had been on that track more or less when the Sixties happened. And of course the Sixties was me. I took to the Sixties like a duck to water. It fitted my soul.

The shit didn't hit the fan till Bill moved in with me and got me to be a writer. I guess this was in 1971.

That is when I quit the school system and became a writer instead. And my parents totally freaked out. As long as I was a school teacher that was fine.

When their friends' daughters became lawyers for the ACLU, they got much bigger dreams for their daughter. Their ideal was that I be a lawyer for the ACLU too.

But my dad had been a school teacher for the school system his whole life, my mom was a school nurse. It was always a given when I was growing up that I would be a school teacher too.

It upset them totally that I was living in the East Village. They didn't know nothing about the Sixties or the hippies, they had no idea that was going on there.

All they knew was I was living in a slum. They couldn't

understand why their daughter was living in a slum.

My tenement apartment bothered them terribly. Once when my dad drove me home from a family gathering, he pointed to the housing project across from my building.

They were co-op apartments that NY State had built to try to keep the middle class in the city. They were very nice with balconies and grass growing around the buildings with benches you could sit on.

Back then I wouldn't have lived there if you paid me. It was identical to what I had grown up in Queens. Except we did not have terraces.

Everyone who lived in them was the same as my neighbors in Queens. They lived there because they wanted to stay in the city, not move to Queens.

But they wanted a nice apartment. It was extremely inexpensive, very affordable. You had to put your name on a list. And when your name came up, you could buy your co-op apartment for $1500 and pay tiny rent too, $100. month.

My father offered to buy me one of those when he drove me home back in 1969.

"No way Daddy!" I said, "I don't want to live there."

I liked where I was living. I was happy in my tenement

apartment, I found it charming.

Of course all that changed when I turned 30. Suddenly I wanted comfort. I had no idea why I had rebelled against sunken living rooms and wall-to-wall carpet. I had no idea why we had turned up our noses at the suburbs.

I wanted to live in the rural country side. I wanted to live in small town in the country side. I wanted to live in the suburbs. I wanted to go back to living in Queens. I wanted to live anywhere except a tenement apartment in the East Village.

I had moved there as a lark, to be bohemian. And now I was trapped there. And I stayed trapped there for the next 16 years. I could not figure out for love or money how to get out.

I couldn't care less about being cool. I had no idea why I had wanted it in the first place. I thought "Look where it landed me! I am trapped in an inner city and can't get out!

"All my cousins live in nice houses in nice places in quiet residential neighborhoods.

"I live in poverty in a slum! I live in a hovel!"

I wanted back the whole life I had thrown away. I became very nostalgic for Flushing where I had grown up.

I think this is why I didn't really take to punk rock when

it broke out in my neighborhood. The last place I wanted to be was in these completely seedy clubs on skid row.

I was 30 years old, all I wanted more than anything else in the world was to live in a cabin in the woods by a lake. All I wanted was the woods and a lake. That was my dream.

Bill was interested in punk rock when it first started. He recognized the creativity. He took me to CBGBs and bought the first 45s of the first bands. And I did appreciate the creativity and their rebellion. I liked their names Sid Vicious and Johnny Rotten. I did like their spirit.

There was a kinship to the Sixties spirit, although the Sixties had disappeared by this time. They were more in your face than we ever were. Our music was not the same.

When we sat around stoned in each others apartment, first we played the Beatles, then we played Ravi Shankar. When you are stoned on pot you can listen to Ravi Shankar forever. It is heaven.

And when we went to Central Park for Be-ins we made our own music which went on forever, with sticks on tin cans. We tripped out on our music. We sure had fun.

May 5th evening

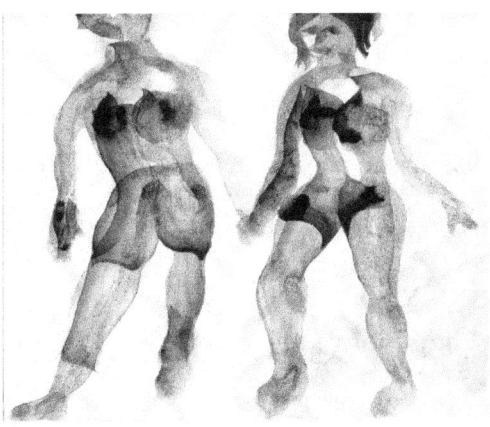

From my higher self

My Higher Self enticed me into taking down this dictation from her by saying she would explain my story about my generation to me. Of course I was curious to hear what she had to say about my generation.

It was in the evening I was lying in bed watching TV, and she said "Go to your computer and I'll explain it to you." So I did.

And true to her word she did begin off talking about my generation. For the first 5 seconds! Then she went way off course…

From my Higher Self

Anne wrote this story of her generation in the middle of telling about her visit with Ryota. The day before she had told the first half of the story of the visit.

She sat down the next morning to tell the second half. Instead she quickly veered off course and wrote about her generation instead.

The following morning she got back on course when she sat down at the computer and finished telling the story of Ryota's visit.

"So I'll just delete this story of the '60s and my old neighborhood," Anne said.

"No I don't want you to. I want you to keep it."

"But why?" Anne kept asking me, "why?"

There was simply no way I was able to explain it to Anne, why I wanted it. Instead we had the same conversation many times.

"I'm just going to delete it," Anne would say.

"No I want it," I would say.

"But why," Anne would say.

"I want it," I would say.

There is no way I can explain to Anne I see value in the

story, she doesn't. She simply doesn't understand her own story and there is nothing I can do about it. She will leave it in because I want it in. Anne does what I want. She trusts me.

Her generation the Sixties generation was looked down on by the generation before them and looked down on by the generation after them.

No one esteems drop outs, and they were drop outs. Many dropped back in, many tried and didn't succeed.

Some never tried to drop back in like Anne. She became a writer and that was too precious for her to give up for anything.

She didn't care about the poverty. All artists want is the free time to do their art. That is their great luxury, free time to do their art.

What she longed for was the countryside, she longed for nature. But there was no way to make that happen. She got stuck and didn't know how to unstuck herself until she found Me and I showed her an easy fast inexpensive way to escape New York.

And once she got out she never looked back, she knew it had taken a miracle for her to get out. She was so so grateful it had happened.

Yes she stayed in New York 15 years longer than she wanted to, but they were also the years of writing. It is when she got serious about writing and wrote every day.

Not really every day, no writer writes every day. But she wrote a lot and when she wasn't writing she always wanted to get back to it. She put nothing else ahead of it, except her husband and their dog.

But when she found Me the year before she left New York, she put Me first. Not ahead of her husband and her dog, they always came first, Anne is a devoted soul.

But she looked to Me for reality rather than her writing. I replaced writing in Anne's life, it was her relationship with Me which gave it meaning, not her art.

When she wrote at all during that year she wrote about me. Discovering Me, the experience of Me. I was what was happening in her life, and she always wrote about what was happening in her life.

When she first moved to Tucson she did go back to her writing. As Anne said "it just feels so good to be doing it."

But 6 months later she discovered *A Course In Miracles,* and then it was bye bye writing.

All she wanted in the whole world was to learn that *Course.* Halfway thru the *Workbook* she came up with the idea to use her ability to write and her comfort in writing, to concretize what she was learning, to make it real for her.

And I would say it helped a lot. *The Workbook* is one lesson a day. And Anne would sit down each day after she did the lesson and try to concretize it for herself. Try to see what it meant. Try to make it real and practical, try to understand it. Bring it down to earth.

Occasionally in the middle of it a really hot story would emerge, some image would bring it on, and the writer in Anne was dying to follow it. It is the gems writers live for, but she would not give in. She wanted to learn *A Course In Miracles* more than anything else in the world.

LOL it was like the biggest fish in the world biting at your line and refusing to reel it in.

LOL she was sitting in the rowboat with her line in the water but she wasn't fishing for fish. She wasn't fishing for a story, she just wanted to make spirit real to her.

And then after she finished *A Course In Miracles* she began to watch television. Nothing interested her till she started to watch the news.

I told Anne the real story is never what appears on the surface, the real story is way below the surface and I would tell Anne what was really going on. And she was fascinated.

And then came that point when she saw her country in peril and she went all out to save her country.

She said "I moved Heaven and earth to save my marriage, I will just move Heaven and earth to save my country."

Anne's experience of saving her marriage was actually hell. You could best describe it as walking thru hell with Me holding her hand. I wrapped her in a cocoon of peace and love while storms raged all around her.

But when the dust cleared she had succeeded. She saved her marriage and had a very deep loving trusting relationship with Me.

It was her ups and downs in her marriage which turned out to be her spiritual path. Because she wouldn't give up her marriage no matter what. Whatever problems came along she was determined to solve. And she did.

With my help.

And I am the first one to say she never could have done it without me, and she never would have wanted to do it without me either. It was all about our love.

Altho Anne was passionate to save her country, her emotions were not involved. She spent all her time, energy, thought on it, but I would describe it as a joyous experience. A thrilling experience. And a major education.

And that brought her to be a poster on a news forum, which she did 24/7 till Bill pushed her to go back to her writing. He had pushed her into writing to begin with. And now he was pushing her back into it.

LOL she resisted with all her might. She was so happy posting on her forums 24/7, having so much fun and communication and play and closeness and love with her fellow posters.

Anne knew there was no longer any real purpose for being on the forum, the country had taken its own unanticipated direction.

Yes Anne had been called at the time, she was called to help save her country. Many were called then and Anne was one of them.

She was not doing anything, all her time was free time, and she had nothing to do. It was a perfect enterprise for Anne. She was made for the enterprise and the enterprise was made for her.

And when the country went in its own direction anyway, she liked continuing to pour out My love to her fellow posters.

That was really what it was all about for her last two years on a forum. Anne became My secretary, pouring out my love. And she loved doing that.

But Bill who has more perseverance than anyone in the world, persevered in trying to get Anne to go back to her writing. She had zero desire to, she was absolutely content on her forums.

But Bill succeeded and again this was a huge favor he did Anne. By then Bill was in communication with his Higher Self who told him "Anne doesn't want to because she thinks she has already written everything she has to say. But in fact she only scratched the surface."

And when Bill relayed that to Anne, the die was cast. She returned to her writing the next day and hasn't stopped.

From first to last, writing was one of the great gifts Bill gave Anne. He got her to start writing a few months after they were living together. It was his idea and he said he would support her.

And he did. He always did. He supported her financially so she could do it, and he supported her emotionally. Anne would never have become a writer were it not for Bill.

There are many great gifts that lad gave her and I would be hard pressed to say which is the greatest one. He brought dogs into her life. And that has been her heart. He gave her a marriage, which was the right marriage for Anne with the right husband. And he gave her writing.

A girl in the pool said to her the other day, "I am reading your books. What an easy life you had! It is all apple pie and ice cream!"

"I didn't have such an easy life," Anne replied, "I left out the hard parts in my books."

And who is to say? That is why there are so many writers. Each describes a different part of life.

Everyone has a life of ups and downs, and the hard parts are usually as hard as the person can bear, because that is when all the learning and growth take place.

About 15 years ago Bill heard a guest on the Art Bell radio show, talking about remote viewing of all things. Bill found his book in the library and took it out and then Anne read it too.

He is probably the same age as Anne, and had his hardest years the same time Anne had her hardest years. Altho he was in the military when it took place. It was during peace time.

He had come from a military family, his father, and grandfather and going way back. It looked like he would have a successful career in the military and then everything went wrong.

His life turned into a nightmare, a long extended nightmare. They locked him up in a military mental hospital just for starting to have ideas which are different from the military ideas.

They wouldn't let him out and he wouldn't back down. But he had a very good friend, his superior officer (who shared his ideas) who stood by him and helped him. And his wife stood by him too.

And when the ordeal was all over, his very good friend, his superior officer, did a long shamanic healing with him in the woods, which cleansed him from all the trauma he had been thru in his ordeal, and let him have a fresh life.

He was kicked out of the military of course, you can't stay in the military and go up against them, but he had his wife and his fresh new life.

It meant a lot to Anne to read that book at that time. "So someone else went thru big ordeals while I was going thru mine. I understand his experience, he would probably understand mine, even tho they are in different departments of our life."

Yes Anne has had her share of ordeals, who has not! But all Anne wants to do is give joy in her writing. She wants to have a good time while she writes it and give others a good time to read it. LOL she is the original good time girl.

Others will talk about in their writing the problems life serves up, what everyone lives thru.

So that no one has to feel alone in having those experiences too.

Her friend Ruthie has just started writing now. And Anne finds it very interesting that Ruthie is willing to go where Anne was never willing to go.

The experiences which cause emotion, the experience of those emotions. Ruthie reads it to Anne on the phone after she writes it, and Anne thinks, "yes that is what it is like, exactly."

Ruthie is Every Woman, they are the experiences all women have. It's not about ordeals, Ruthie doesn't write about ordeals. It's just the experience of life as lived in the emotions. It is really quite interesting and Anne hopes Ruthie will continue.

Every writer who is honest has so much to offer. And each is as individual as the individual herself. And each is priceless.

Writing is not about talent and not even about creativity. It about baring your soul. And each chooses to reveal about herself, what gives deep pleasure and gratification to do. And it's never the same.

No writing could be more different than Anne and Ruthie. But Anne sure hopes Ruthie will stick with it, because she learns about herself and her life when Ruthie reveals herself and her life. That's the way it works.

Anne does limbo rock on her honeymoon

May 8

A story about nothing at all...

Cupcake is lying flat by the tree out my window watching the birds. They are all pecking at the can of yesterday's cat food I put in middle of yard.

Cupcake and Priscilla ate what they wanted yesterday. I opened up new can for them this morning. And yesterday's half eaten can I put in the yard for the birds, who love it.

What seems so interesting to me is that Cupcake, who is a huntress, and who usually watches the birds from secret hiding place ready to spring into action. Now she is not.

In fact as I look more closely her ears seem to be pointed in my direction, she is not aquiver as she is when she is hunting. I think she is taking a nap.

O no I am wrong, she is facing toward the birds watching, but she is not hunting. She is too relaxed. And not at all in position to run and leap.

LOL she is watching the birds the same way I lounge on my bed and watch TV. She is having entertainment.

Lounging on the sweet ground in the sweet cool morning air. She had her breakfast. Now she is having her lounge and the birds are supplying her with entertainment. Something to look at as she lounges. I have TV, Cupcake has the birds.

O she did spring into action! I guess one of the birds alit so low down in that other tree she actually thought she could get there. But the bird was too fast for her. They always are. It's the sparrows. And they are fast flighty birds.

So she changed her spot to under the sun couch where she is more hidden.

My yard is full of sparrows now. And now that she has left her spot next to tree right out my window they are all back in the tree. It is my favorite tree and theirs too.

They are having fun in yard this morning.

Well life continues in its speed-up phase. I don't think it is going to slow down again till the Mass Awakening actually happens.

Even tho every summer before this has been long slow

monotonous, I just can't imagine this summer being that way. Since all we have been having recently is more speed-up.

In between each speed-up seems to be 4 days of rest when it is almost impossible to pull yourself out of bed in the morning. When you wake up the first thing you want to do is go back to sleep.

You spend those whole 4 days saying to yourself "who knew it took so much energy to get out of bed!"

Then after that rest period, the new energy arrives, and it is so much faster than what was before. So much happens in your life and it all happens so fast.

Life turns into one happening event after another.

You say to yourself "How can all this be happening! I have a life where nothing happens."

Nothing seems to stay the same at all. I am talking about habits. One day I am fascinated by all the news on TV,, can't get enuf of it. And next day after two seconds I switch to entertainment channels.

My activities at the computer change. After months of ignoring my blog, suddenly every morning I am working on it. Posting new stories, new pics. Learning how this new updated changed blog actually works. Google has changed everything.

When things slowed down momentarily in the middle of last week, I said to myself "OK, I will learn how it works. The key is patience. Instead of trying to rush thru everything, I will take all the time in the world and learn how to do it."

I gave Jim a whole day off, I didn't go swimming. I gave myself a day off. I spent all morning learning how the new blog works.

And by the end I had mastered it. Not totally I am still learning. But I did get to post a few new stories up there. I was back in business.

And I had a better attitude on the long weekend evenings this past weekend when nothing was on TV that I wanted to watch. As usual I kept changing channels trying to find something.

As usual I finally gave up. But I gave up with a better attitude. "So it means you're going to be bored! So what! Your days are so happening now, a long evening of boredom may be just the ticket. It is how you rest up so you are prepared for the next day."

I even made improvement in my problem of putting myself down. One morning I woke up in a bad mood, waking up in bad moods can happen a lot I notice. But they don't last long. I seem to balance again after an hour.

But when I noticed myself having a hostile thought, I said to myself, "So what! Let it go thru one ear and out the other. Putting yourself down for it is worse!"

I actually succeeded in nipping *putting myself down* in the bud.

I am actually getting better at this when it comes to the minutiae of daily life. When I spill things or knock things over, or have a thought I don't think I should be having.

"So what!" I say, "no big deal!" I am really trying not to put myself down relentlessly for everything I think or say or do.

What a miracle that would be if I could get off my own back!

Some thoughts are deeper and more problematical for me. Their content upsets me. Disturbing memories.

Sometimes they come in a slew. Ranging all over my past.

Sometimes it is one big one which knocks me for a loop.

But I deal with them best as I can. If it is totally serious and totally threatens my happiness, I remind myself that nothing ever happened, it is all just a dream, and I have been sleeping in Heaven all this time. And I will wake up soon and be happiest girl in the world.

When it is just flotsam and jetsam from the past, coming in a slew, like logs down a river, I just say "stop thinking about it, the past never happened, turn on the TV, there's probably a show you will like."

If they barely upset me at all, just minor disturbance, I say "maybe it is a good thing, they are coming to the surface to be released."

In the end no matter which type it is, I always turn on the TV as a solution to take my mind to another place.

I decide that thinking is not working out for me.

May is the haboob

On May 9th the haboob came to Tucson

Harry was leaving work to come home when it arrived. Here is his email about it:

I too had quite an experience with the haboob.

It hit really hard when I was driving out of downtown on my way home.

I had never been in anything like it.

As dense as the densest fog, but hard driving wind, whipping the car back and forth!

And the color of orange dirt. Weird.

The wind kept up, but it got clearer as I got closer to home.

May 10th

My big cousin John

Well my long day of doing nothing all day yesterday took it all out of me.

I woke up this morning to blue sky and sunshine ready to greet the day, ready to have a happy and full day. I sat down at my desk lit a cigarette looked out the window and think "I am dying to go back to bed."

Who has the energy for today. It took all my energy to get thru yesterday.

It's like needing a vacation after you get back from vacation.

My big cousin John went back to New York City for his vacation last fall. And when it was over he needed a big vacation.

Better him than me. Maybe the boy cannot get enuf city.

Like me he was born in Manhattan. But his parents never moved to Flushing, they just moved to a bigger apartment in Manhattan. He did go to out of town college in a small city in upstate New York

But instant he graduated he was back in Manhattan. He went to graduate school at Columbia, studying his father's field, psychology.

The instant he obtained the advanced degrees so he could practice it, he married his girlfriend, and they moved to San Francisco.

And at first all their trips back to New York, they stayed in that huge apartment with his mother that he had grown up in, all their trips back were nurturing.

You go back to see your old friends, you see your family, you are back in your hometown. You have gone back home.

You wake up in the morning to all the familiar sounds of the cars beeping on 96th Street, and you think "home, I'm back home." It is all about returning to the much loved familiar.

I guess New York is still home to you after you first leave. It takes a while for the new place to turn into home.

When I visited John and Ellie out there 5 years later I

asked his wife about the change. They had toddler son now, so John was away at work, I was sitting in the kitchen with her.

Ellie said, "It's different than New York. Here everyone is so busy. They have coffee with you for 15 minutes and then get up to leave for their pottery class or macramé class or yoga.

"No one sits around and schmoozes." After 12 years with my cousin John she had picked up some Yiddish.

She was not native New Yorker like we are, had grown up in Atlanta, had become a stewardess and was based in Manhattan.

Which is how she had met my cousin John. Four stewardesses were sharing an apartment together on the East Side of Manhattan.

This was back in the summer when my cousin John was 22, staying in his mother's apartment when she was vacationing in Greece.

I guess he was dating stewardesses then, and when he was introduced to Ellie that was the one which took.

They began dating and you could say they never stopped. I think she was a year older than him.

She told me soon after "I always wanted to marry a

Jewish man because Jewish men like to talk."

I guess she wanted a husband who would have a lot of conversation with her. I have no idea? I was 18 years old, all I knew were Jewish boys from NYC.

Maybe the Atlanta boys she had dated before she came to NYC didn't like to talk. Or the pilots she met during her first years as stewardess. Or the Upper East Side boys her stewardess friends introduced her to.

All I know is practically in my first conversation with her, when we were first getting to know each other, she said "I always wanted to marry a Jewish man because they like to talk."

She was completely happy with my cousin John. She was a knock out and every single man in my family, all my uncles, all my boy cousins, had a crush on her.

She was the dream of every man in my family.

And she was so nice and so easy to talk to. She really wanted to fit in in the family. She went all out to be nice to everyone.

But as soon as she and John actually got married, even tho his mom had given them a nice co-op apartment as a wedding present, he let his kid sister have that nice apartment, he and Ellie took off for San Francisco.

I don't think she wanted to leave New York. She had fallen in love with it. But New Yorkers always want to leave New York.

And he had fallen in love with California the summer in college he had spent out there. I guess he chose San Francisco as the city they would move to, little New York in California.

I can't imagine my cousin John in LA. He was born on Riverside Drive like me. Then the family moved to West 96th Street. Then when he got an apartment of his own after college, it was on Riverside Drive and 96th Street. Then when his mom gave him that brand new co-op apartment it was on 96th Street between Amsterdam and Columbus.

A boy who has spent his whole life on West 96th Street in Manhattan doesn't move to LA. He moves to San Francisco.

He is used to being in a city with all nationalities, he is used to a big China Town. He is used to a city which is a port.

And where museums figure prominently.

He is used to living high up, the part of Manhattan where he lived was high up on Riverside Drive. He is used to all those steep hills and river close by.

And walking to the little stores to do all your shopping.

Ellie, who had grown up in a house in Atlanta, said let's buy a house. And she found an old Victorian house which needed a lot of work in the Haight Ashbury neighborhood they were living in. And his mom bought it for them.

It was very inexpensive then. And Ellie did all the work herself.

When I visited 5 years later she was still painting the bathrooms on the second and third floor.

Ellie married him because she said Jewish men like to talk, but in my whole life I think my cousin had probably said 18 words to me. If he is talkative I have never seen it.

I guess he is talkative with Ellie. He is not talkative with anyone else in the family.

But he is a very nice guy. It was hard to see when we were all growing up because he always had a shell around him. We are a very talkative outgoing family, and he wasn't like that. In our family of Big Mouths John never had a big mouth.

But I know him a lot better now than when we were growing up. The man has a very sweet loving heart.

Ellie really did get a nice husband for herself. Plus he is willing to talk to her, none of the rest of us seem to have been able to get him willing to talk to us. He has always been a good listener instead.

But a listener only goes so far. At some point you want the other person to express themselves, so you have a chance to get to know them. And that I have never had with my big cousin John.

There is closeness because we both went thru the worst day of our life at the same time. He was in New York visiting his mother in the hospital, at same time to the day, that my beloved first dog went to Heaven.

When he couldn't stand spending one more minute in her hospital room, I guess all the relatives were there. The hospital was so close to my apartment, he said "I'm leaving, I'm going to see Annie."

My dog had gone to Heaven early that morning.

Bill and I had taken care of everything. Now I was back home. He had gone to the handball courts to try to cheer up.

I think I was lying on my bed sobbing when the downstairs bell rang. I was sobbing out to God "Why couldn't I save her! I tried so hard to save her. I wanted to save her."

No one could have done more than I did to save my dog during the previous two and a half months. To say I moved

Heaven and Earth to save her is an understatement.

If I am sitting here right now a totally different person from who I was until the vet pronounced that death sentence on my dog two and a half months before, it is because of the total and complete transformation I went thru in that two and a half months where I spent every instant of it trying to save my dog.

Maybe that was what I was sobbing when the downstairs bell rang, "I tried so hard to save her."

I got off my bed and said "who's there?" and he said "your cousin John." John of all people! What a stunner! I hadn't seen or talked to him or heard from him in 15 years and we had barely known each other.

My house was a mess and I was a mess. I think when I started sobbing, I wasn't even lying down. I was just walking in circles in my tiny tenement apartment, sobbing and throwing up at the same time, "Why couldn't I save her! I tried so hard to save her!"

I had just two minutes till he climbed the 4 flights of stairs to arrive in my apartment. I had to choose whether to clean up the throw up and sobs all over the floor, or change out of the mess I was in.

I wiped up the floor and answered the door.

He was so beautiful in all his expensive clothes. So starched and clean and beautiful. I was still in the mess I had spent the previous 24 hours in.

"O John" I instantly said when I let him in, "my dog just died." Back then I didn't know we all lived forever. I still thought death was real.

And he instantly took me in his arms. My aloof cousin who I barely knew, instantly took me in his arms. The mess that I was against all those fancy expensive starched clean clothes.

"I know how attached you were to her," he said.

He took me in his arms. And said "let me take you out for a cappuccino and cannoli."

Mine was an Italian neighborhood.

He took me to a fancy neighborhood café for a delicious iced cappuccino.

I couldn't believe I was sitting in such a pretty place, with my beautiful cousin, drinking something so delicious and wonderful.

It was such a nice respite. Especially from where I had spent the previous 2 and a half months. Either in my apartment with my dog, who was looking worse each day even tho I was hoping beyond hope.

Or my friend George would arrive and carry her down the stairs and up the stairs because she liked being in the air outside. And we would sit at the stone table in the playground across from the precinct where all the homeless hung out, and George and I would play cards.

George always looked like a ragamuffin but he loved my dog and my dog loved him. George was my best friend in the world for what he did for my dog and for me when our time of great need came.

But now my dog was in Heaven, or what I thought then, was no longer alive, what I needed most at that moment was to be in my own cousin's loving arms. I needed all those fancy beautiful clothes he was wearing, and being taken to that lovely sparkling café.

John did good for me. When we left the cafe he didn't go back with me. Instead he walked up those few blocks to where the hospital was, where his mom was. His ordeal was not over yet. Mine was.

I realized afterwards we had saved each other. After night and day in that hospital room, he had to get away. And saving me was just the ticket.

We each needed that pure loving closeness as he held me in his arms. And we probably both needed that lovely iced cappuccino together in that lovely café.

We both needed huge change in our surroundings. In a place of pretty and sparkling. And we had our love.

So you can understand about John and me. I thought we will be close and loving from now on after that. But in fact instead we had the same relationship we had always had before. Zero contact whatsoever.

But 25 years later when Bill went to Heaven, he was the only one I called. I waited 3 days, and then that evening God said "call your cousin John and tell him."

And John was great. I wasn't upset like I had been about my dog 25 years before. I knew now we all live forever and it is just a change of address and Bill is perfectly happy.

But still it was the biggest thing to happen in my whole life, and it meant my whole life would change.

As attached as you are to your dog. I didn't know it back then, she was my first dog. For me losing her was the end of the world. But in fact you do get another dog, and in time your whole heart belongs to her. The heartbreak heals, and you are heart whole loving your new dog.

You have a heart full of happy love again. Your new dog is the love of your life now.

The joy of your life, the happiness of your life.

But a husband is irreplaceable. You are a single girl now and will be for the foreseeable future. It is no longer our home, our life. No more *we*. Your partner is somewhere else. Your helpmate. He isn't with you in the world. He's at his new address.

Yes you can communicate with him all day long and all night long. You are never away from his love. Never away from him. But your life in the world is not the same.

John was great when I called him. He stayed on the phone with me for two hours. No more rushing me off the phone in 5 minutes like he always did before. And he understood me perfectly.

He understood how and why I could be high and happy even tho this big thing happened. He understood my friendship with Jim and how he helps me, how we kid around.

John laughed at the things which made me laugh too.

Yes he was concerned, I could feel it. He didn't know how his little cousin would manage on her own when she always had her husband to take care of her. And she no longer had her parents to help out.

"Jim offered to teach me to drive."

"I think you should start your lessons right away."

I really didn't want to and God had not said I had to, but I asked God while I was on the phone with John.

"Hold on, let me ask God."

And God said "good idea, start to learn to drive right away."

So I told John, "God said 'yes, start right away.' So I will."

And with that we got off the phone and I felt so much better after talking to my cousin John and letting him know the big thing which happened in my life.

"I'm not telling anyone in the family," I said, "you tell them.

"They won't understand me. They won't understand that I am happy. They will send me condolence cards saying I'm so sorry for your grief.

"I don't want those cards and I don't want those phone calls. It is a miracle that I am happy and I want to stay that way."

I guess it was a miracle phone call. It was just what I needed. God did a genius thing to have me call my cousin John at that moment.

I did need all the warmth and intimacy of family then, I was too alone. And John is the only one who could possibly understand and he did.

Despite his concern and despite the earthshaking change it was for me, we spent a whole hour laughing together on the phone.

And another hour having a wonderful conversation filled with communication and understanding.

It is probably the greatest phone conversation of my life.

Which is why I can't make such a fuss that he hasn't called me for chat for 20 years.

May 12th Saturday

Haboob

Well we are definitely in another phase and I know which day it came in. It came in with the haboob Wednesday afternoon.

That huge wind blew, definitely the strongest wind I ever remember. I took 3 steps out of the house and it blew me back into the house.

I closed my front door and it shoved it open.

I put something heavy to keep it shut and it shoved it open thru that.

It knocked over huge and heavy things in my front yard. For us it was a dust storm too. There was almost no visibility while it was going on.

The cats refused to be outside in it. The morning had been very chilly and overcast, and blowy. They both have such long luxuriant fur they reveled all morning in that very chilled air.

It was almost as if they were saying "At last you got it right! This is what we like."

Mid May days are usually uncomfortably warm when you disport a huge fur coat from tip of your nose down to your toes. The sun is too hot for them.

But instead they had everything they liked. It was way too chilly for me, but delicious for them.

I even think they liked it that it was so overcast and dramatic. It changed their world in the backyard. They even might have liked those strong breezes, the wind which was making the trees dance, everything was in motion.

Even tho my cats have total freedom, they can be outside whenever they want, they don't go far afield. For a little kitty cat my backyard must seem huge to them, for them it must seem like acreage.

They find the front yard more interesting because there stuff happens. Neighbors come in and out of their house.

And the cats like lounging on top of the cab of my truck or on top of Jack's car when it is parked in my driveway and he is not around to notice.

So I think the unusual weather we had all day till the haboob arrived in late afternoon made it all adventureland for them.

But a wind which is so strong it blows me back into the house after I take 5 steps outside, would be a tornado for little lightweight cats. Their bulky shape is due to their very long very luxuriant fur.

That wind would have blown them all the way to Kansas and then up to Oz.

And my life has simply never been the same since. It has stirred longings in me that are so deep I don't know where they come from.

It's as if there is a pool or well so deep inside us we never knew it was there, until the haboob came in on Wednesday afternoon and blew everything on top of it away and stirred it to its depths.

I spent all Wednesday evening in that longing, all Thursday evening, and all last evening too.

I don't know if it will ever go away now. Three evenings in a row of such intense longing. They don't wait for evening to come in. They seem to arrive at 4 pm, same time the haboob arrived on Wednesday, and continue till I finally fall asleep around 10 pm.

So it is long lasting. 6 hours of it. Sometimes I fall asleep in the middle of it. I get some respite that way. And have intense dreams.

But it is an intermission. I do a few little kitchen chores and then find myself right back in it.

Interestingly when I wake up for an hour or two in wee hours, when I am up from midnight to 2, I don't have it.

And I never seem to have it when I wake up again at 6 the next morning.

It just blows in in the very late afternoon and is almost unbearable. It wouldn't be unbearable if it weren't so long lasting.

There is no way for those desires to be fulfilled. You experience them as coming from some part of you which is way below the world, altho it could be way above the world, you just know it is not in the world.

The love and intimacy you are longing for doesn't exist in the world. But seems to be a memory. What I mean is you seem to know with your whole soul that it is something you once had, and lost, and now you want it back.

You want it back passionately. The longing is tremendously intense.

The feeling of emptiness of not having it is unbearable. As if a huge gaping hole opened up in the middle of your life.

It is the loneliness which goes with it which is unbearable. You keep checking your email, but there are never any emails when you are going thru it.

You keep switching the channels on the TV hoping for something to take you out of it. But the world of TV is too remote for you.

You go out and get the mail and your neighbor Jack is driving his car into your driveway at that instant. He sees you looking at him from the screened window and waves to you. And you both say loving words to each other. And that helps.

During that moment which love passes between you, you are out of it. The longing and the intensity of the longing disappear for that instant. Because it is a longing for love.

Later you look out that same window and see your cat Priscilla lounging herself on top of Jack's car. And that pleases you, again there is an instant of satisfaction.

Nothing on TV is capable of doing anything for you. None of those pictures on the screen. They all seem so unreal. But Priscilla lying there so comfortably, spreading herself on top of his car, looking so happy there, that sight pleases you. Pleases your soul.

So I guess the whole thing must be about what the soul likes. Love passing between you and Jack satisfies your soul. Seeing your cat Priscilla high up on top of his car looking so happy there, it is a spot she loves. That sight pleases you.

And for the rest it is all torture.

6 hours of trying to get thru intense feeling.

Every hour or so you get up and go into the kitchen. Where you find yourself saying, "this is killing me, this is torture."

"Do something!" you implore God, "do something. I can't take it."

"You have to do something!" you order God.

They are all outbursts of desperation.

Sometimes the desperation takes another form. You just give up.

"I'm not even going to check my email," you say while you are standing in the kitchen.

"There won't be anything. There never is anything. And I don't care," you whistle in the wind.

"I don't care that my life is empty and lonely. Who cares!"

This is the point when you have given up. You are no longer imploring God or ordering God or begging God. You have decided there is no hope.

Sometimes you sit at the computer smoking a cigarette and say to yourself "what is it that I want so much?" And you realize you want to be loved, you want to feel love.

And this is so close to the bone, and seems so impossible in terms of what the world has to offer, that you go back to looking for distraction.

"I'll begin fixing the typos on the story I wrote Thursday morning," you say to yourself.

The story was so intense, probably if you weren't going thru what you were going thru, you'd never want to face it at all.

I don't think that story of my cousin John would even have been written except it was the first morning after the haboob blew in.

It was where you went that first morning after the haboob. Much to your own surprise. It was the last story you ever expected to tell.

But it was born out of that first evening of longing for

intimacy. The evening of the haboob.

And each evening after that, when the longing is so intense you can't bear lying on your bed another instant, you say "OK I'll go in and fix the typos."

It really doesn't bother you to face the intensity of the story because of the state you are in. Anything is better than experiencing that pure intense longing with no hope of it being fulfilled.

And it turns out there is no distraction from it at all, except fixing the typos on your intense story.

And so now you know all about my life right at this instant. How the haboob came in 4 days ago and blew me away and I haven't been the same since.

But yesterday morning I had a wonderful morning. My first time of wonderfulness since haboob blew in.

In fact my first time of wonderfulness for a solid week. Because the days before the haboob were car trouble and mornings after were car trouble too.

But yesterday I had wonderful time in pool and when Jim picked me up in Mustang afterward, it drove like a dream.

He did succeed in getting it fixed. And it was so much fun being back in a convertible again and driving like a dream. Being in a sports car instead of my old truck.

"Take me to my Navajo jewelry store," I said when I got in the Mustang.

"I want to get my bracelet fixed and my necklace fixed and I want to get myself a new ring.

"The lifeguard liked my ring, and I was finally able to prevail upon her to accept it.

"So now I have one finger free, I want a new ring."

And O that was so much fun. I haven't been back to Mac's Indian Jewelry since November.

There is nothing in the world as wonderful as walking into an Indian jewelry store knowing you are allowed to choose something beautiful for yourself.

"I didn't bring my purse with me," I told her, "so I can't pay for anything now. But let's choose a new ring, and when I pick up the bracelet and necklace I can pay for the ring then."

She was so wonderful and I loved her so much. And what is as wonderful as that wonderful lady, looking at all the beautiful rings in the case, and choosing which she thinks are beautiful and trying them out on your finger.

There were two we both liked. "Put them away for me," I asked." When my necklace and bracelet are fixed, I'll come back and choose my ring then."

And when I got out of the jewelry store I was walking on air. All my happiness had surged back.

It was just so great to feel like life was worth living again. That life is great. That life was delicious and wonderful. And so much fun and made out of delight.

I think Jim was happy to see me so happy again. To see me back on top of the world. He likes to see me happy.

And he drove me back home in the car which ran like a dream. And it was so nice to be taking a different route and be in a different part of town than we always are in.

It's amazing that the buying of new Navajo ring can do that for you.

She shops..

May 13th Sunday 6 am

My higher self helps me with my feelings

Help arrives

For past week my feelings have been so intense. It's been like an unbearable longing. What I am longing for I don't know. It began on Wednesday with the haboob and on Sunday morning when I sat down at computer my Higher Self said "I'll help you."

I write down her words as She says them to me

OK maybe it is time for a chat.

So many feelings, such intense feelings, such a sea of feelings.

Are they trying to tell you something? What are they trying to tell you? Are feelings just like the weather. An environment you live in, a changeable environment.

One day the weather is too hot, next day too cold, next day just right.

So does the weather mean anything, do you take it to heart? Must you take your feelings to heart. What is their meaning, what is their purpose, or they just are.

Does it matter if they are more intense some days, or more intense for a morning. They are changeable. Very changeable. As changeable as the ocean.

It is like living inside the ocean, to live inside your feeling. Filled with tides, pushes and pulls. Moving in and out with the moon. The moon moves so rapidly and pulls the ocean with it.

Fish swim with the tide. They let the tide carry them. They never swim against the tide. It would be impossible.

For a fish tides are natural. It is all they know and all they ever have known. For them tides are the way life works. Life without a tide is inconceivable to them. Life is made up of tides.

And my darling Yes it is here now, in the middle of the Sign of the ocean, the Sign of the fish. Is it any wonder you are overwhelmed with feelings. The force of them on you is so strong. You are so pulled by them. They are pulling you along. Resistance is futile.

Trying to buck the tide does you no good at all. It just scares you because you feel the full force of the tide when you try to go against it. You experience its power. Better to swim with it. Let it carry you along.

Yes it moves you from one place to another. Tides are always going somewhere. It is the exact opposite of stagnant, even the opposite of stable.

You can't expect stability when the ocean currents are this strong in your life now. And the ocean currents are feelings. The currents of feelings, strong currents of feelings. Deep and strong feelings way beneath the surface.

And so my sweet, maybe let's take it all a lot less seriously. Where it is taking you we do not know. Just that it is taking you. And where you will wind up you don't know. It could take you to another shore. A shore far far away from where you left.

Honeybunch let's not be panic stricken swimmer floundering in the ocean, overwhelmed by the current and the tides. The ocean carries you. That is what it is meant to do.

It is so vast and it carries you. You're such a lightweight to it. It takes less than a finger to carry you. So why not lie back and let the ocean carry you. Whether it is the ride of a lifetime, or the gentlest of raft rides, or some of both.

Raft rides on a gentle ocean is what dreams are made of. People used to dream of the sea.

Honey let's just take it easy. It won't always be such a sea of feelings, such intense feelings. They blow in, they will blow out. Signs change. But each has a gift for you. And the gift of this Sign is feelings.

Maybe you can't stand them right now, they have been so intense, day after day. Not so many days, it just feels forever. It's only been 3 days or 4 days. It's only been half a week, not even a week. It's been half a week.

And not even all day. An evening or a part of an evening. Or maybe a late afternoon.

It's not the time, it's the intensity, and that they re-occurred the following day. And because they lasted for a whole hour which is a very long time.

But they have a purpose, all these feelings, all this feeling, all this water. It is how we wash the slate clean. It is a cleansing, a big cleansing, a super cleansing. It is taking a bath.

That is what it really is my darling. A very big very long bath. And as long as you don't confuse yourself with the bathwater, you will be fine.

Sure everything is in the bathwater now. Everything which has been washed off, washed away. It was deep cleansing, and you are amazed at what is now in the bath water for you to look at.

"So what happens now" you wonder, "do we pull the drain, and all of that goes down the drain. Or is it just washed and purified. And returns to my mind and heart, remains in my life, continues to make up my life.

"Or when this bath is over and I emerge from it, it no longer goes with me. It has been washed out of my hair.

"No matter how attached I was, that's what water does, it unglues the glued.

"Maybe I don't want to give up my attachments. I was so attached to my attachments. But I'm not sure I have a choice about it. The water has unstuck the glue.

"They are swishing in the bath all around me now. The choice is mine, I can stick them back on when I get out of the bath. Or hold them in my arms and kiss them goodbye.

"Give a great thank you for all they gave me. And set them free as I set myself free.

"O lord it hurts to let go. It feels like a wrench. But perhaps it's just for an instant. Like the instant prick of needle when it goes after splinter. Just an instant of wrench.

"Well we shall see what we shall see. Where it will be when it's over I don't know. This particular ocean voyage."

Thank you Higher Self for everything.

Love, Anne

The next morning

Feeling good again

It feels good to feel good again

Cupcake is up in the tree. It's a thrilling sight. She is coming down now. O she just came down. There is nothing as beautiful as watching a cat climb a tree.

The good news is the week of intense longing and intense feeling of emptiness which came every evening for a week, did not arrive yesterday evening.

I felt happy and was my regular self all evening. I emailed with friends and that was a joy.

And I loved their emails back to me.

And then completely happy and completely satisfied I went in to watch TV.

Which was very pleasant.

Love, Annie

May 18th

Dream last night...

Anne has opinions

I was up at 2 am again. I stayed up till dawn and then fell back asleep. I didn't watch TV, I tried, but nothing interested me.

I got up and read some of the political news on internet. None of it was interesting but it must have affected my dreams. Because when I did finally fall asleep for another hour at dawn, the dream I had before I woke up was about politicians.

I dreamt Bill was here and we were chatting.

He said "I want to ask you your opinion."

I said "You don't want to hear my opinions, you never like my opinions of people in politics."

I thought he would ask me about people we had already talked about and had hot disagreements.

But those were not who he asked me about.

First he asked me about Hillary.

I said "nice girl, works very hard, is sincere."

Then he asked me about Ross Perot.

I said, "I like him. He's fun. He has a mouth. Jesse Ventura has a mouth too."

I always like people with a mouth. It's fun. I never had a mouth myself. I don't know how they do it.

No matter what you ask them or throw at them, they have answer right there.

It's probably a dream about me and Bill.

I am the girl who is sincere, a nice girl.

He is the one with the mouth. Which I found so much fun. He made life interesting for me…

Bill

Every few months for a solid week I dream my husband is back home and we are having conversation together again. It's nice being back with Bill having conversation. I always did enjoy his conversation.

Bill is a very nice guy. He is sensitive and loving to every living being. To the animals, to the plants, to the insects. He saved the birds when they flew into the house and got trapped here. He saved the huge bumble bees when they were in house and couldn't find their way out.

He also had an impy side which made life fun and lively for me.

He is friends with the bird

Bill's impy side

Bill's cartoons are at billstampone.blogspot.com

Part 2

Life changes gears..

May 26th

I enjoyed my driving lesson today so much...

LOL I haven't done any driving in so long I forgot where the pedals were. When I saw stop sign coming up I was flummoxed, I had completely forgotten how to stop.

Both Jim and I (it turned out) had been up at dawn and both Jim and I (it turned out) had fallen back asleep and slept till 11 am.

I had gotten up and written a story when I discovered I was up at dawn drinking coffee and feeding my kitties. I knew I had nothing to say and nothing to write about but it passed the time.

I was waiting for a movie to come on at 9 am when I must have closed my eyes, and when I opened them it was almost 11 am. I was so surprised

I came into my computer room and sure enuf there were

2 phone messages from Jim, but the first one was at 10:30 so I knew he had overslept too.

The plan had been today would be the day I would start to face driving in traffic. But of course when I woke up in a total daze at 11 am that was out of the question.

Jim was in a daze too. His idea was drop me at my pool and go on to his pool and wake up in the water.

But driving has been postponed so often and for so long, I knew today was day I had to do it.

So I suggested he take me to countryside where there is not another car on the road. I think I wanted to get out of town too.

"Let's go to Corona Road" I said when he arrived 15 minutes later. "You fill up the truck for me on the way and wash the windows and mirrors from all the wind. I'm in a total daze and I can't move."

He didn't want to wash the windshield after he filled up the truck, but he did it.

He himself drives all the time with windshield and mirrors a total mess, it doesn't bother him at all. But I knew I had completely forgotten how to drive, I wanted visibility on my side.

And I really did perk up when he washed the

windshield. It made me feel like all systems were on go.

At Corona Road we changed seats and I put a fluffy pillow behind me so I could reach the pedals.

I didn't have to think about how to start the car because as soon as I sat down it started on its own. It was moving along slowly even tho I had no feet on any pedal.

So I was driving before I even started to drive. I drove along in first like that and then switched to second, by now I had foot on gas pedal.

But stop sign arose shortly and that is when I realized I forgot how to stop.

But I was relaxed and happy as I was driving along until I got near stop sign. I had forgotten that I enjoy driving.

"I forgot how to stop" I said to Jim.

"It will come back to you" he said.

And of course it did.

And I made nice turn, very smooth, went along that road, very smooth, made next turn very smooth, and then I was on that road I forgot its name, heading towards Swan Road out in the country.

Swan Road out in the country is my favorite road. It is long road which arrives at dead end, perfect for me, a maximum of 3 cars on the whole drive.

When we reached Swan I pulled over so I could adjust the pillow behind me. It is always uncomfortable but usually I am too tense when I drive to bother. But this time I thought "why not be totally comfortable."

So I leaned over so Jim could adjust the pillow so it was actually behind my back, not the usual lopsided way it is.

And then relaxed and happy I drove the whole long distance on Swan Road in 4th gear.

Jim had wanted me to go to 4th gear on Corona, but no way! I didn't want to switch to 4th when I was amazed I was driving at all.

I was happy driving along and said to Jim "I love driving."

He said "you have something else you love beside swimming."

I said "you got it."

I was driving so effortlessly and well that Jim said "you must have a good driving instructor."

That's how I knew I was driving well, because he was complimenting himself on how he taught me.

On the way back on Swan, I said "I'll go on that dirt road."

I was just about to open my mouth and brag "I am such

a genius I know exactly where that dirt road is," when Jim said "you passed it."

"When? Where?" I said.

"All the way back there" he said.

"O" I said.

So I did a lovely U turn, maybe that is when Jim said "you must have a good driving instructor."

And he pointed out the turn-off to the dirt road.

Instantly it was so rough and I was so jostled that I thought "this is big mistake, I don't want to be here."

But for some reason Jim thinks driving on dirt roads is good for me.

And then I discovered the huge advantage to me of driving on that very bumpy dirt road in the middle of nowhere.

I didn't have to look at the road at all. I could look out the windows at both sides and drink in all the beauty.

It was so much fun driving along at 15 miles an hour just looking at the desert with mountains behind it on both sides.

"I love it," I said to Jim, "I can go as slow as I want."

He said "the speed limit here is 35, you are going 15, you can be tagged for driving too slow."

"Get outta here!" I said. "What sheriff is going to give me a ticket for driving too slow on a dirt road in the middle of nowhere on Saturday morning of Memorial Day weekend!

"If the sheriff comes along and he is cute I'll just go and make out with him."

"I'll drive the truck home for you," Jim said.

"Alice has her navy seal," he said, "you can have your deputy sheriff."

"I'd rather have a deputy sheriff than a navy seal," I said.

Alice doesn't have a navy seal in real life, that is malarkey I cooked up for Jim.

She was invited to be in an art show in Mexico several months back, and when she got back she told me on email a navy seal who is also a painter was there and said he knew a gallery which would take her paintings. But it didn't work out.

But when I told Jim the story I said "she is bed with her navy seal and she won't get out of bed."

"Alice is one hot chick," I said to Jim.

I was so relaxed and happy driving on my endless bumpy dirt road, the only car on the road, looking out the window on both sides, drinking in beauty of desert, that for first time I looked in the mirrors.

"I looked in my side mirror and I could see behind me," I told Jim.

He said "if you look in the top mirror you will get broader view."

Usually I am so tense and nervous driving that looking in the mirror is totally beyond me.

But not on the dirt road this morning. I looked in the top mirror for very first time in my whole life and I found it so interesting the big broad view it gave me.

I was squealing with delight.

He said "you can look in the passenger side mirror too."

I looked but I didn't see anything. He adjusted it 3 times and I still didn't see anything. I just saw regular desert.

I didn't see any road.

He said, "It's good if car is coming up alongside you, you can see it."

I said "OK why don't you get out and run along side of the truck while I am driving and pretend you are a car and I will look in that side mirror and see if I can see you."

Poor Jim what he has to put up with putting up with me! It never crossed my mind for an instant that he thought

I was being serious.

He actually thought I wanted him to get out and jog along side the truck and pretend he is a car so I could look out that side mirror and see if I can see him.

"What?" he said.

So I looked him straight in the face and said it all again and I had just about reached the end when he called out **WHOA!!**

I guess even when you are going 15 miles an hour on a dirt road in middle of nowhere you have to pay some attention.

When he called out **WHOA!** like that I turned around and saw my truck was way off the road and was starting to climb the embankment.

"I guess my truck loves you" I said, "he acted up when I said you had to run along side it while I looked in side view mirror."

And as soon as I said it again, truck swerved and went wicky wacky again.

There is no other explanation my truck must love Jim and doesn't want me to come up with ideas for him which make him faint.

When I was coming near the end he said "you can do

your U turn here," and I did exquisite U turn.

I didn't think I had enuf room but Jim said "you do." And after all that practicing the 3 point turn I can make very tight turns.

Of course I aced the U turn on dirt road.

And I guess that is when I discovered I was in bliss. I began to stretch myself luxuriously and languorously as I was driving because the bliss was just suffusing me.

I've been in bliss sometimes recently in my swimming pool, the lovely water, the lovely air, the lovely sunshine.

But not while sitting up in drivers seat of truck. It just felt so good, stretching around in bliss.

I was so happy.

"I'm so happy," I said to Jim.

And then the little paved road I was on came to a real road with cars whizzing by.

"Let's change seats," I said, "you can drive me home."

"But you're supposed to be learning how to drive in traffic, you're supposed to be driving on a road like this."

"Naw" I said, "being in bliss is just too wonderful. I'll learn to drive in traffic another day."

I really think I made the right decision to switch seats when I was still in state of bliss. And just enjoy Jim's exquisite driving while he drove me home.

I was still walking on air when I got out of the truck in my driveway and thanked Jim for my wonderful lesson.

I know I'm not progressing in my driving at all, but as I said to Jim "who cares, being in bliss has value too."

June 3

The day I knocked everything over...

LOL Anne was a mess all day

A cloudy streaky sky. Such a gift that all these cooling clouds arrived at same time as our great heat.

I woke up yesterday morning before sunrise and thought to myself "is it possible today is overcast and cloudy!"

It seemed like such a miracle. We have not had overcast and cloudy in months and months. No one in Tucson last remembers when we had it. We have had flawless blue sky and intense bright brilliant sun forever.

The idea of cool damp cloudy overcast is so refreshing when heat and light are great and TV had been flashing heat warnings all over the screen.

It wasn't a total fantasy of cloudy overcast. Some of it was real. When I opened my eyes all the way yesterday morning and looked out the window it wasn't darkly overcast, which had been my wish of the day.

The dark was because dawn had just started to break. The light hadn't risen yet.

But I had not imagined the clouds because I got the huge treat when I looked out the window of seeing them all filled with pink.

We never have pink in our sunrises and sunsets unless there are clouds. It is the clouds which turn pink.

And with no clouds at all forever and ever I had forgotten about pink sky at sunrise.

Instead we have had that exquisite breathtaking beauty of crystal clarity. Light starting to dawn in a night sky when it is crystal clear is not about color at all. I don't think there is any color. It's a beauty without sensuality. It's just awe. You are transported into miraculous beauty.

So yesterday was a horse of another color. You wake up to dream of cool dark cloudy overcast, and dare I say wet, and open your eyes to this pretty pink sunrise. As pretty as a party dress. It was huge treat.

And it was lovely cloudy and slightly overcast all day.

And this morning is another one. I tried to feed my kitties and give them fresh water and put up my coffee with dispatch, so I would be all in place sitting here looking out the window for when the sunrise tuned pink. I wanted to see it again. I wanted that treat.

But sunrises are like a fast action film. You really can't say I want to be in place to watch another pink sunrise. It's just a miracle that you were lounging on your bed looking out your window when it happened the morning before.

Sunrise is so beautiful, every sunrise, all sunrises, maybe in June they happen faster. It was already light outside when I arrived at my desk with my cup of coffee, lit my cigarette, and clicked on God's Letter to all of us for this 3rd day in June.

I forgot all about the sunrise when I read the first

paragraph. Because it was a love letter beyond all love letters.

Yesterday was a totally peculiar day. But it seems all my days now are peculiar in one form or another. Who knew peculiarness had so much variety to it. That there is so much range in peculiarness.

There are as many different ways days can be peculiar as there are fish in the ocean.

And there was such a variety of ways my yesterday was peculiar.

I really didn't do anything. I was up at crack of dawn as you know. And then 5 or 6 hours later Jim called, and he took me to my dress store to return the two dresses. And then took me swimming. Then he picked me up and took me home.

And after that I did not step one foot out of the house except to get my mail. And the phone never rang and I did not get even one email.

So it was just me alone in the house with my 2 kitties all the livelong day. And all the long evening too.

The first peculiarness was the extraordinary clumsiness. It was literally not to be believed. It turned the whole law of averages on its head. I literally could not move a muscle without bumping into something, knocking something over.

Everything which could be spilled got spilled. Everything which could be dropped, got dropped. Everything which could get knocked over got knocked over.

I really don't understand it. No one gives full concentration to your routine movements around your house.

But it was like "while the cat's away the mice will play." If my mind was away and how could it not be, I was spending whole livelong day doing intense concentration on the computer.

Teaching myself how to crop Bill's cartoons and increase their resolution so I can put them in my new book. And scanning new ones, so I could have an assortment to choose from.

But that doesn't explain why every instant that I wasn't doing that, each time I got up to do anything, pour a cup of coffee, give a snack to my kitties, go in to watch some TV to take a break.

Every single thing I touched or even went near, or even breathed on, fell over, spilled, broke, dropped to the floor.

By the end of the day I gave up. I had already spilled my orange soda all over my cigarettes, my little nail scissors, my cigarette lighters.

Every time I got off the bed I spilled the water bottle and the glass filled with water.

When I put the ice cubes in a small bowl so I could set my soda in it to keep it cold, not only did all the ice cubes fall over but my soda did too.

The only thing I managed not to do is overturn my dish of food on the bed while I was lounging there eating it while watching TV.

Any liquid I went near spilled. But the food stayed in its bowl.

Finally it must have been 11 pm by now when I decided to get out of bed to help myself to another Hershey bar and I overturned both the water bottle and tall glass filled with ice water.

I no longer registered surprise. I thought "it couldn't be any other way."

Once something has happened 1000 times in one day you don't believe it could be any other way. By now you know you can't make a move without overturning something.

TV was just not that interesting, so after 10 minutes I would decide to go back and give it another shot learning how to crop those cartoons.

Naturally I managed to knock over, spill, drop, bump into, and break everything between my back bedroom and the computer room.

I don't remember when I decided to finally close up shop and give a real try to find something I could enjoy watching. But when the movie was too boring I would mute it, turn my head aside and think.

And I think that is when I first noticed that every thought which had come into my mind had been a negative thought. I can't explain it. It was like being in a mosquito infested mind. Every thought was discouraging.

I had finally gotten one email late in the day. It was a spread sheet of my sales report. It showed that zero people had bought zero of any of my books for past year.

"No one reads my books. No one is interested in my books. How come no one likes my books!"

"No one calls me. No one emails me. How come I have no friends!"

It was like the theme song of the day.

Every instant that I wasn't concentrating at the computer

or momentarily paying attention to what was on TV, it came into my mind in all its endless variation.

"I used to have friends. People used to want to be my friend. How come all my old friends lost interest in me."

Then I'd get up, spill everything over, and go back and scan some more cartoons and try to actually succeed in cropping one.

But when I closed up shop for the day and went in for serious TV watching and that didn't work, so now I had all the time in the world to think, it took a turn for the worse.

I sank to the bottom.

"I'm so lonely. I can't stand it."

But then a movie came on which actually caught my interest. *I love you Alice B Toklas.*

And it was so much fun watching Peter Sellers be a Jewish lawyer in Los Angeles during the '60s with his Jewish parents. All that Yiddish, even some words I had forgotten about.

And his mother so upset when his brother, the hippy, shows up at the funeral in his hippie outfit.

"What kind of meshuginar outfit is that!" mom says.

"Who wears their Indian suit to a funeral!"

Naturally a family fight breaks out at the funeral.

"I am expressing my belief," her son says.

"This is what Comanches wear to a funeral," he says about the feather on his head and the war paint on his face.

Altho it was fun watching his parents inadvertently get stoned, my favorite parts were before. When they were the typical Jewish family, being so familiar to me, the world I grew up in.

Reacting to everything the way all parents did back then. Whether they were Jewish or not. It was just that Yiddish got mixed in with all their reactions which made it even more delicious for me.

It is funny, here I was longing so much for family, for my family. I wanted that warmth and intimacy. Of course there is no way for me to have it in real life.

But I guess all it took was Peter Sellers with his Jewish family in L.A. to give me what I wanted.

Because I clicked it off when I realized the rest of the movie was Peter Sellers going hippy and I was content with what I had watched.

I fell asleep with a smile on my face and even woke up happy this morning. I had woken up out of sorts for the past 4 days but woke up sorted out this morning.

Maybe these long days in the house do accomplish

something. It doesn't seem to matter whether I spend them in a sea of bad thoughts.

The next morning I wake up with a clear head. All of the mishegoss which used to be in my mind just isn't there.. And that is a pleasure.

She holds up her can of orange soda

June is happy month

On their way to the Big Top

June 5th

Anne switches pools

My friend Mary is so welcoming

The early morning sunlight is turning the leaves of my tree chartreuse. I am looking into green lit up radiant chartreuse. I am looking out at chartreuse light. It's pretty.

It won't last more than a minute, the sun will climb higher in the sky, but it sure is pretty right now.

Lacy green leaves made up of chartreuse light.

The rest of the trees in yard are still in shade. So this is just a luminescent centerpiece.

The birds are full of delight. They love this cool early morning. They are having a ball playing together in my yard.

I guess I am happy. Everything just feels OK.

Things seem to have climaxed with that huge full moon in wee hours of yesterday morning.

Before that I was working up a storm. Where the energy came from I don't know. Maybe from that gathering full moon.

If it is strong enuf to pull the mighty ocean, then I guess it can do the same thing for me. Night and day I was at my desk working on my new book.

A huge surge of energy. Then full moon climaxed and I stopped.

LOL I rode the wave. I scanned 30 of Bill's cartoons, and spent tremendous effort learning how to crop them. Hours just slipped by.

I remember thinking at one point or at a few points "I am spending two hours trying to figure out how to crop this cartoon."

But then I thought "So what! What else do you have to do with your time! You're doing this instead of watching TV."

I guess all my TV time was spent at the computer, scanning and learning how to crop.

TV became something I would watch for 10 minutes when I decided to take a break.

But it wouldn't hold my interest. 10 minutes later I would go back and tackle cropping again.

I never aced it. Each one took 2 hours, I would try and try. Finally I would decide to give up. But even after I said "I give up!" the temptation to try again was too great. And usually after 3 tries past the time I decided to give up, I would get it.

So that is how I spent that tremendous full moon energy. I liked it.

Lizzie, the head lifeguard at the Y pool, also overworked during that time. She simply never stopped working. It was like looking at mirror image of me. Except all her activity was in the swim pool, mine was at my desk.

But yesterday the full moon energy was maxed out by sunrise. I actually got to see that huge full moon set as dawn began.

And yesterday was not a work day. I did not do a lick of work. It didn't occur to me to work. I had zero desire to. It didn't interest me, it didn't pull me.

Jim took me to Grocery Outlet on the way to the pool yesterday, where I bought potatoes, rice, tuna fish, and coffee. Just exactly what I needed, why I had him take me to grocery store to begin with.

Sure I would have liked to look around. Check out their cookies, their perfumes, their pretty dishes.

When Bill drove me I did all that. But with Jim waiting in the hot convertible I did none of that.

My husband didn't mind the heat and he would listen to the radio. And he was willing to indulge me because he was my husband.

Jim won't listen to the radio when he is waiting to save on the battery. And he hates the heat. And he's not my husband. He is a friend doing a favor. Different rules apply.

Also because I don't have my husband to lug the groceries into the house for me when we get back home, I want to buy less to make it less of a burden for me.

So really it all worked out perfectly. I was in and out of the store in 10 minutes and there were not that many bags of groceries.

So Jim continued on Craycroft to Fort Lowell Pool.

The Y won't let us swim there for the whole month of June. They turned over the two hours of morning lap swim to swimming lessons for children.

I had a fit at first. I said to Lizzie "How can you tell us we can't swim for a month! Can't the water aerobics ladies give up one of their hours for us?"

She said "No, because 35 people show up for water aerobics and only 3 of you show up for lap swim."

I don't think it's fair to go by the numbers, and I still think it is wrong.

But I knew in my heart everything happens for the best. Fort Lowell Pool is closed in winter but open again now that it is summer. I knew it was time to show my face over there. I have friends there.

And I haven't shown my face at Catalina, my other pool, for a year either.

And I have friends there too.

After I chewed Lizzie out for kicking us out of the pool for a whole month, I said "It's OK, Heaven has decided it's time for me to see my old friends at my old pool.

"I wasn't doing it on my own, so Heaven arranged it."

She was relieved I changed my tune at the end.

Her defense, "it's only for a month," is a joke. A month is an endless time in the hot desert summer to keep you out of the pool.

The solution of course is to go to the public pools during that month. And I was so relaxed, comfortable, and happy at Lizzie's pool I never would make the push to go back to my wonderful public pools.

But of course yesterday I did. Because yesterday was the first day of the Y being closed to us swimmers.

Which is why Jim just drove down Craycroft to Glen where Fort Lowell Pool is and deposited me in the parking lot.

"At 1 o'clock 400 day camps arrive in their busses, pool is bedlam, so pick me up at 1," I said.

Jim had suggested I just pay the $1.50 each time to swim, but my Higher Self said "Buy a pass for the whole year. Then you never have to think about money when you arrive at the pool.

"Plus it means if the Y is ever closed for any reason during the year, Jim can just drive on the extra mile and take you to Catalina.

"You'll feel secure knowing that a pool is always available to you no matter what."

At the pool

None of the lifeguards who are there this summer know me and I don't know any of them. This is a first for me.

But I had all the time in the world and I took my time writing out the check for a pass for a whole year.

When Jim had taken me on Mothers Day to Ross to get bathing suits on sale, the only 2 left in my size were both skirt suits. It wasn't what I planned on but turns out to be very convenient.

Because I can put it on before I leave the house, just put a blouse over it. And I look like I am in a summer outfit, blouse and short skirt. I can wear my bathing suit for going to store or credit union.

So first I bought my pass. All I had to do was pull off my blouse and dive in.

The water was a lot colder than at Y because Fort Lowell is such a very deep pool.

I discovered my addiction to very deep water is over. I immediately swam over past the lines for the laps to where it is a little shallower.

The Y pool is so very shallow and so very small, and has no view at all, which is why I didn't like it at first, after being a regular swimmer at Fort Lowell.

Where the pool is so very deep, and so huge, and high up. And spectacular view of the mountains and huge sky.

But as Bill said about the weight room at the Y, "It is my

favorite because it is so cozy."

And that's what happened with me over time with their pool. It became my favorite because it is so cozy.

I just became so happy with my Y pool, which was always so warm, and only had two other people in it beside me. And luxurious hot shower afterwards.

At first the water seemed chilly and so deep and the lap lane seemed so long after my tiny Y pool. "How am I going to stick this out for an hour and a half until Jim picks me up?" I thought.

It's for serious swimmers doing their workout, and I am neither a serious swimmer nor do I work out.

My way of swimming is just to dream myself along the lane.

So first thing I did was to move out of the very deep water to where it was a little shallower and where the distance is shorter.

LOL I shortened the lane and made the water shallower so it was more like what I was used to now. And then I liked it. I got used to the water, it stopped being so chilly. And of course I do love to swim, it makes me happy.

So I was actually completely happy swimming along.

And then I looked up and saw Jack and Mary sitting on

the bench outside the shower room. I thought "Durn I missed them! They are leaving just as I arrived."

So I swam some more. But when I looked up next, they were both getting into the pool. So I realized they had just arrived.

I looked up and Jack noticed me and waved. And I waved enthusiastically back. He must have said to Mary "Anne is here" and she waved too.

But instead of just standing on the side of the pool in the water talking to each other as they used to do in past summers, they were swimming together.

I guess because Jack finally taught himself how to swim 3 summers ago, they no longer have to stand up in pool and talk, now they swim.

My Higher Self said "Don't go over, let them swim."

So I went back to my own swimming. And I was enjoying it. It felt good.

And then at some point my Higher Self said "OK go over now."

I was shy to because it looked like they had just taken a short break and were swimming again. I swam a little more and my Higher Self said "Go over now." And this time I listened and swam over.

And the first thing Mary said was "I didn't come over right away because I wanted to do my exercise."

Which of course was fine.

And at first we stood up and chatted the way we always did. But now that I realized Mary can swim and likes the exercise, I said "we can chat and swim at same time, that way you can get more swimming." And of course she wanted it.

I really don't know how long I got to chat with Mary. All I know is she looked at the clock and said "I want to get out before the gazillion kids arrive," and to my shock it was just a few minutes before 1.

I didn't want to be naked under the shower when the kids arrive, because they stare and point and laugh and bring their friends to see too. It is big event to the little girls, the naked ladies under the shower.

Plus Jim was coming for me at 1.

I really had a nice time chatting with Mary. It has been forever since I have chatted with someone who is a friend and shares my interests.

At the Y I chat with the lifeguards who are all in high school or college. Or with Nancy who does her exercise routine in the water, we both love mystery books and mystery shows on TV and we talk about that.

But I notice when the lifeguards talk to each other they have a real conversation because they are the same age and share the same interests.

And when I see my friends at my former pools, is when I get to have a real conversation.

Mary is on the identical wavelength with me and shares the same interests. Which means we can communicate about many things.

Like everyone else she is too busy to write more than a one sentence email. Altho I always do enjoy her perception in it. I appreciate her emails.

But how totally luxurious after a year of short and sweet emails, to have a whole half hour long wonderful conversation.

I guess that is the trick to everything. It turns out everyone but me is too busy to email. But swimmers always arrive regularly at the pool for their exercise. They are there for one hour and are always up for conversation.

And eventually you become friends with all of them and best friends with some of them. The friendship all takes place in the pool or under the shower.

If they are serious swimmers like Kathleen it takes place

under the shower. If they are like Patty and Mary, they prefer to shower at home, but Patty swims with her head out of the water, we chat as we swim back and forth in the lane.

And Mary and I can too.

It was just nice to have conversation back in my life. Conversation with a friend. And I love Mary and she loves me.

It was such a treat.

I hadn't realized what a rich diet I was on when this was my life with Bill. Day in day out we went to the public pool, either Fort Lowell or Catalina. And day in day out I had conversation with friends there.

No wonder I never missed my old friends from NYC and longed to have conversation with them. I was having conversation with my new friends all the time.

It really worked out perfectly. Because Mary and I had traded email addresses last year, I was able to update her about my life as it went along. And even tho her emails were short and sweet, it kept us close, and I was able to get an idea of what she is up to now.

She has just started a little business, selling the beautiful jewelry she makes on the internet. I sure want it to work out for her.

But after only making $27 in toto for all my books all these past years, altho Mary may be disappointed her business isn't taking off right away, "How is your business going?" I asked yesterday, and she made a face.

But look at me I don't make a dime, and yet how wonderful to have projects to work on!

She designed the gorgeous brochure. She set up her site. She advanced her design skills on the computer. And she has the adventure of starting an enterprise.

It was also fun talking with Mary yesterday in the pool because of her brilliant perception. Whatever I said she had a comment on it. And it's fun all that brilliance.

Usually it was one sentence comment à la her emails. But also à la her emails each one is brilliant. It is just that I had whole half hour in the pool instead of rare emails.

It's fun confiding things to someone and knowing you will be understood, which I have with Mary. But it is even more fun when she does talk. I love brilliance. I wish I could describe Mary's brilliance. It's always one sentence, or mostly, but it's like popping in a kernel of truth.

Brilliance is fun but it doesn't compare in any way, shape, or form to love.

The first thing she said when she first swam over to me was "let me give you a hug." And there is no heaven like being hugged by Mary. All that love.

And many times during that half hour of being together our love emerged and that was really nice. I guess that's what it's all about. Love, there is nothing like it...

June 13

I fix up the truck

Cupcake is in her yard. She is just sitting there looking. There she is, sitting on the ground. She turns her head in one direction and she sees something she wants to look at.

But mainly she just sits there taking in the early morning

air which is still so cool. She isn't really sitting up and she's not lying down. She's on her haunches.

It's the bird call which interests her so much. My yard is alive with bird call.

O now she stretched out her front legs, her back legs, and is slowly walking toward the house. I can't really tell where she is going because she walked out of view of my open window.

But it is nice sight to greet my eyes when I first looked out my open window. Cupcake in her yard, taking the air listening to the bird song. Swiveling her head when she wanted to look in different direction.

Her vibe matches perfectly the early morning dawn on desert.

O I think the sun must be rising now. It must have reached just peeping over mountains because the light has reached the tree out my window.

The leaves are translucent green. And the sparrows arrived in it. It is a beautiful sight when the light first hits the tree. It glories in the light. Hahaha it is glorified in the light.

My glory tree.

My wonderful chartreuse glory tree.

But it is the bird call which is the star of the show. It always is. That's what's going on. That's what's always going on.

I just love it. You hear all the chirping in the nest, but calling out loud and sharp is that call. I wonder who makes that call and where they are. A constant murmur chatter in the trees and then occasionally that loud sharp distinct call ringing out beyond everything.

The day before yesterday an hour before sunset Manuel, Frank's brother-in-law, brought back my truck. It looked like a brand new truck, I never would have recognized it.

It had been so pathetic looking when he arrived with his helper to pick it up. We had bought it brand new 20 years ago, two months after we moved to Tucson. I no longer remember the shiny beautiful red it was when we first got it.

Our desert sunshine is so intense that after day in day out in it for 20 years, it was so faded and sorry looking. It had one tiny dent Bill had put in it, and it was always his dream when we won the lottery to have that dent taken out and have it repainted and new upholstery.

The seats had worn through, the springs were coming thru on the drivers side.

It didn't get really beaten up until I began my driving lessons last year. The huge long scratch on one side when I tried to pull out of my driveway for the first time and gas meter was too close. It just ripped all the way across.

And then all the scratches and dents when I was learning how to reverse. Capped by the catastrophe when I was reversing way too fast when I didn't know what I was doing, backing up very fast, and crashed into the fire plug in corner of my yard.

That did it. After that my truck looked like shit. The whole back corner of my truck was way dented, it took out the rear light. It just made a hash of it.

It meant never having to think about locking up no matter where we went, because no one in the world would decide to steal it. Nothing could look less appetizing.

There were minor things inside which had been broken before I began driving. They were made of plastic and just not lasted. Both door handles had broken off, you had to put your hand out the window and open both doors from the outside.

When I told Jim I wanted to have the dents taken out and have it repainted, he said he knew a few inexpensive body shops, and what we do is take it to all of them to see what price they give us.

But Frank told me his brother-in-law does it in his yard. And my Higher Self said "Just go with Frank's brother-in-law."

So Frank drove the truck to his brother-in-law. And told him the whole story of him and me to inspire him to give me a good price.

Frank had been renting the house across the street for the past 5 years and because Bill spent all his time in the front yard he and Frank had gotten to know each other very well. They were friends.

But 2 years ago Frank moved down the block.

I hadn't even met Frank except the few occasions when he still lived across the street and his dog would run into my yard and we would wave hi to each other as he called his dog back.

But the morning Bill went to Heaven, Sharon was walking her dog Shiva, I had never met Sharon before.

It was just an hour after dawn broke and I had stepped into my front yard to throw out some stuff and was standing there drinking in the most beautiful early morning there ever was. When Sharon came over with Shiva to find out what happened. "My husband just went to Heaven" I said.

And she said "so did Frank's brother." It turned out that Bill and Frank's brother had woken up in Heaven at the exact same instant.

"It's just a change of address," I said to Sharon, "we all live forever."

And she said "my husband is at change of address too."

And for some reason that made me bust out laughing. I laughed so hard I did a little dance. At that instant there was more love and closeness between me and Sharon than I had ever experienced with anyone in my whole entire life. As I was laughing and dancing in my yard and hugging her and looking at her with such love.

I knew then Sharon was my angel. She had come to me when I needed her. She saved me. She and Shiva her dog were two angels sent by Heaven to help me.

And after that I went in the house to call Jim to tell him about Bill and he said "be right over."

I said "take me to the Circle K for coffee and donuts, we can have them in my back yard."

And when he arrived I walked out with my arm raised in triumph and a smile all over my face. A happy girl. And I thought "let it be remembered that an hour after my husband went to Heaven I arrived with a smile on my face."

Of course I don't take credit for it. From the instant it happened God simply wrapped me in His arms, raised me so high, smothered me with love. I was in a cocoon of love and raised way high above the world.

And I knew that my mission was to demonstrate that no matter what life throws at us we can hold on to our peace and happiness. Which is exactly what I did.

I glowed.

And the instant I got in the car with Jim I began teasing him about winning all our bets on football games.

"When football season opens" I said, "I will win every bet and then win Super Bowl too," I said.

I kept this up all the way to the Circle K a mile away and on the way back with our coffee and donuts which we had in my backyard with my doggie.

Finally he couldn't take it when I went too far. "I will win every bet because I know football and you don't know football at all."

This amused me no end because I knew Jim had played for our football team the Arizona Wildcats.

He said "No way will you win every game!"

My nail polishes were sitting on the table in front of us as we drank our coffee.

"Yes I will," I said, "because I will vamp you."

I pointed to the purple nail polish in front of us called Vixen.

"I will wear my vixen nail polish," I said.

"It won't work" he said, "I am immune to it."

"Then I will spray on my perfume" I said.

"I am allergic to perfume" he said.

I can't believe he is proving to me I won't win every bet in football, I thought to myself.

This must be a first. Bill was his good friend, he is sitting with his friend's wife an hour afterward. And he is countering every idea I have for vamping him so I will win every bet in football.

He's proving to met I won't succeed in vamping him.

I was delighted because I knew it meant Jim and I were solidly on the path to happiness together.

And then he got down to brass tacks. "The first thing is I will teach you how to drive."

"OK" I said.

"I'll get you the Drivers Manual now so you can begin to study it. And then I'll return in 3 hours to take you swimming."

"Thank you Jim" I said.

"Learning to drive is easy" he said, "I can teach you in 5 minutes."

"Thank you Jim" I said.

I didn't win every single football game but I did win most of them, including Super Bowl. For a girl tuned into Heaven it was easy for me.

It drove Jim crazy because he knew I had never watched a game and didn't know how it was played and hadn't even heard of most of the teams.

Bill was a fanatical fan so I knew all the teams he talked about. I knew all their names. But Jim went wicky-wacky when I won the bets on the high school teams since who knows the names of all the high schools in Arizona!

Except for Jim who played for the high school team here and has been to every Tucson high school game since then and watches the Phoenix games on TV.

The first high school game was on Friday night in September.

That afternoon coming back from the pool I said "tell me the names of the two teams playing."

He said two high schools I had never heard of.

I asked my Higher Self and my Higher Self said one of those names.

So I said "Hamilton will win."

LOL he was astounded. "They were only the State champions last year!" he said.

And I thought "WOW I am going to have a ball with this." Which I did.

It didn't take 5 minutes to teach me how to drive. I am still having my lessons now but I have made a lot of progress.

It hasn't been 5 minutes, it has been 15 months. But it is how Jim and I became best friends, got to know each other so well, and Jim picked up some Yiddish, a language he had never heard of and didn't know existed.

Because each time I lost control of the car I would call out "Oy gevalt! Oy gevalt!" until I got the truck under control again.

"Oy gevalt" Jim would greet me with big smile on his face the next morning when we would have a follow up lesson.

So last month when I went to Bill's bank to take out all the money he had there, I decided I would use it to make all his dreams for his truck come true.

Of course at that time he had no idea I would batter it up so much. He just wanted the one tiny dent he put in taken out, repainted, and new upholstery.

It's a much bigger job now. I put the check his bank gave me in my credit union. And two weeks ago when I asked Frank about his brother-in-law doing the job, he drove the truck over to his brother-in-law to find out how much.

He told his brother-in-law all about me and him so his brother-in-law would lower the price. Which he did. Frank came back and said it would be 800.

And my Higher Self had me tell him "That is very kind and generous of him, I will give him 1000. 800 for the job and 200 for tip for being so nice to me."

And the next morning She had me ask Jim to drive me to credit union. Where I withdrew 1000 in cash. My Higher Self said "Give Frank's brother-in-law the money in cash, it makes it easy for him not to have to go to the bank to cash the check."

Frank had said "you give half now and half when the job is done."

But my Higher Self said "Give it all to him when he picks up the truck."

She also said "Get it all in small bills because stores in

Tucson won't accept any big bills to pay for things. This will make it easier for him to spend the money."

I told the girl at credit union the whole story. "I am making Bill's dream for his truck come true. And Frank's brother-in-law will do it for me and I want to give him cash for 1000 dollars and it has to be small bills."

I said "I don't need to watch you count the money. I know you will do it right. Just put it in an envelope for me so I can hand it to him."

And Jim stopped on the way to the pool so I could put the envelope with the money in my house and not have it in my purse while I swam.

I had planned to have the job done the next week. But Jim said "Why wait! He may have another car coming in."

And when I got back from the pool by a miracle Frank called. I said "Tell your brother-in-law I have the money for him now. Whenever it is convenient for him he can come over and pick up the truck."

And an hour before sunset they all arrived. Frank's truck is in the shop, so he arrived in his girlfriend's car. And then there was another car.

I was introduced to Manuel his brother-in-law. The others stood at a distance and watched.

But when I said "let me give you the money now." I said "I didn't watch her count it out but you will want to count it for yourself to make sure it is all here. It is 800 plus 200 tip for being so nice to me."

And I handed him the envelope.

And instantly they all stood at the bed of the truck where Frank counted it out in front of everyone.

I stood a little distance away but they all were close up and watched intently.

Because Frank did it all in a system.

I wasn't close enuf to see exactly. But it seems like he counted it all (out loud) into little piles. Maybe 10 piles of 100 each. Then (out loud) he counted up all the piles. And it was pronounced it was 1000. And the money was given to Manuel. Because he has to pay his helpers too.

And then I showed Manuel where we had put in the brand new back light, but the clips had broken, and could he find clips so he could put it back on for me and it doesn't dangle loosely. He said he has the clips.

Then he said "what color do you want?"

I had planned to ask for navy blue. But I asked him. "Which color do you like?"

And he said "White. Muy bonita."

So I said "Perfect! I want white muy bonita."

And then he showed me where the inside door handles were broken off and he said he can fix that for me. And I was so happy.

And then the whole caravan took off. The two cars and someone driving my truck.

Altho before they left and before I got to thank Manuel so very much for what all he was doing for me, I noticed one of his helpers.

I had been introduced to him when they all arrived. But he had stood in the background the whole time except for the counting out of the money.

Manuel was so young, even younger than Frank. But the helper was around my age. And I realized he had been watching me the whole time. I guess they all had (all the young men who were there too) they were curious about me.

But whereas Manual was all work, he was taking on a big job and wanted to do it right, I knew his helper, my age, had connected to me. It was just a look that passed between us as he stood off some distance in my front yard watching it all, taking it all in.

But it was a look of perfect understanding, perfect

friendship. Perfect connection. Our wavelengths had joined. And love passed between us. It wasn't romantic love or attraction. It was understanding and connection. It was nice.

And the day before yesterday, also an hour before sundown, they all came to bring me back the truck. And what Manuel did for me was spectacular.

There are no words for my truck's beauty. For the magnificent job. It looks like a brand new truck. Jim had to lock it up when he drove to the club after taking me swimming.

Who would not want that gorgeous gleaming white truck which looks brand new! Why it should also look ten times the size beats me.

Manuel is a magician.

It is impossible for me to recognize my old truck. Each time I get a glimpse of it in my front yard, I wonder whose truck is that, who does it belong to. What is that brand new gleaming white truck doing in my front yard.

White muy bonita.

June 18

Yesterday's driving lesson

Is this the girl Jim dreams about meeting in New York City

We had a driving lesson yesterday morning. It was a lot of fun. It was my first lesson, my first time behind the wheel, since truck came back from the shop (Manuel's yard). And the first in my brand new gleaming white truck.

The only thing Manuel was not able to succeed in doing for me, altho he tried, was replacing the seats.

Altho sitting behind the wheel in it again for the first time, and Jim driving it out to Corona Road so I could practice my driving, I got to notice all the little things inside Manuel had done for me.

It's not only that he replaced the door handles which had broken off on the inside.

But the plastic crank which opens and closes the window. Half of it had broken off, it was very hard to close my windows. So I always left them open even when it did rain, which it does occasionally on the desert.

And Jim noticed he had fixed the little door to the glove box. Bill had it taped shut. Whatever mechanism would keep it shut had broken, but somehow Manuel had replaced it. The huge duck tape keeping it shut was no longer there.

I'm not so sure I will rush out and get the seats

reupholstered first thing as I planned.

I may wait a while till I get used to my brand new white gleaming truck. Because the only thing familiar looking about it now are the seats. Worn thru and the springs coming out. (Manuel had tried to replace the seats for me, but could not find one.)

So I got back out all the pillows I had been using on the seats. The 2 skinny ones to sit on, one for driver and one for passenger.

And the fat plump one I use for when I am driving to put behind my back so I can reach the pedals.

Except for the lesson I had the weekend right before Manuel picked up the truck, I have not been behind the wheel since I flunked my road test back in the first week in April.

It has been 2 months without driving. But as Jim said "it's like riding a bike, it all comes back to you."

I was nervous at first when we first arrived at Corona road and switched seats. I got behind the wheel and discovered it had all fallen out of my mind. Which pedal for which and which gear for which.

Jim had told me to practice shifting gears while truck was in my driveway. And I said I would. But when I confided to him when I first got behind the wheel that I had not. He said "of course not."

I guess he is starting to know that I lie.

So before I started driving up Corona Road I shut off the motor. Because I realized if I left everything running the way it was when Jim got out to change seats with me. And I sat there re-finding the pedals, pressing on each one, and shifting thru all the gears, the truck would just take off.

I learned the hard way to shut off the motor before I did all that. And I put the parking brake on too for good measure.

And after that I slowly got rolling up Corona Road. But it all did come back to me very fast. And to give Jim a thrill I immediately switched to second and then to third.

I would have been happy in second, but Jim is always proud when I go to the faster gear, and disappointed in me when I won't.

He himself drives in all the traffic in town in the very fastest gear.

I would have been happier driving along Corona to the stop sign on Alvernon in my lovely 2nd gear and drinking in all the beauty around me. I hadn't been out of town in a month. And it's spectacularly beautiful.

The day before there had been thunderstorms on the other side of the mountains, and altho we hardly got any rain, we heard the thunder.

But that rain, after having zilch rain at all for months and months, was like an incredible blessing from heaven.

It instantly cooled down the tremendous heat. And because I had forgotten what rain was, it was a miraculous new thing I was discovering.

It was so sweet and wonderful and for the first time in memory all the scent of the desert plants filled the air.

I forgot that nature is not just beautiful to look at, but also has a lovely perfume to delight you.

And delight me it did!

I couldn't get enuf of it, I drank it all in.

But during the night the storm had moved on, the clouds had cleared. Jim and I both woke up to tremendous beauty and tremendous heat.

Would he want to take me driving in this huge heat? But as soon as I sat down at the computer, my coffee was completed brewing but I hadn't yet gotten up to pour myself a cup, he called. It was 7:15 am.

"Want to go driving?" he asked.

"Yes" I said.

"Be there at 8 o'clock," he said.

"Perfect!" I said.

"Let me make my coffee now," he said.

"OK I'm going to drink my coffee now," I said.

He yawned all the way to Corona Road and could not wake up for love or money. But when you have been driving forever you can drive in your sleep which is exactly what Jim did.

The TV had warned of scary heat, so I used the time to get 3 cold cans of soda out of frig. Fill up bag with ice cubes, put the cans of soda in there and zip it up.

Get out a quart bottle of frozen water from freezer. It had been in there for a week, it was frozen solid.

And because the Jewish bakery I discovered the day before when Jim drove me there, also makes cannolis, I couldn't resist buying one with all my other pastries.

"A cannoli!" I said to the girl. "I haven't had one since I left the East Village.

"Are they real cannolis? Do they taste like cannolis? I thought only Italians know how to make cannolis."

"He is Italian," she said.

"But this is a Jewish bakery."

"He's Italian and Jewish."

"Great!" I said and I got two of them.

One I handed Jim when I got in the car plus some of the bakery cookies, he loves them.

The other I had her put in the box for me along with my danishes.

I assumed Jim had already eaten his the day before, so I brought mine to give him for a snack while we did driving.

I said "This is a cannoli. It is Italian. It's different from Jewish pastries, not as sweet.

"But you have to get to know them because when you go to New York City and meet a girl you like there, she will expect you to invite her out for a cappuccino and a cannoli."

"What is cappuccino?" he said,

LOL Jim is dying to go to New York City and meet all the New York girls. And I thought he was all prepared now that he has picked up so much Yiddish from me.

But if he has no idea what cappuccino is and has never heard of it I realize I have neglected his Italian education.

He has to know what a cappuccino and cannoli are if he wants to invite girls out in New York City.

So I drove along Corona Road to the stop sign on Alvernon. I remembered how to stop. I turned on Alvernon and again went to second and third to please Jim.

And then a long road I love which takes me to Swan Road, my favorite of all the roads because I am the only car on it.

I really would have liked to go slower and feast my eyes on the beauty, but to make Jim happy I switched to 3rd and then to 4th. The boy is so proud of me when I drive in 4th gear.

He wanted me to step on it to make the light but I thought "Who cares! It's such a short light. Why have all that suspense when I can be so relaxed and happy!"

And I was totally happy looking around while I was at the red light. In fact I forgot all about the light till Jim said "your turn."

It had turned green without me noticing, and I remembered from the past it is only green for 3 seconds.

Instantly I switched to first and started up and thank god it worked. When I go a long time without driving I don't know what will work for me and what won't at first.

I stayed in 3rd this time because I didn't remember how far it was to turn off to Swan Road.

I had completely forgotten how to signal but I did my best. I really didn't think I should be driving that fast when

I made my turn onto Swan Road, but I did it.

And now I was back on my beloved Swan. "What are those birds?" I said as I saw huge birds to my left.

"Buzzards" he said.

"BUZZARDS!" I said. "They are a famous bird. I've always heard of them but I never saw one. They have a bad reputation."

I realize now they figure in prominently in the *Loony Tunes* both Jim and I watch at noon. There is always a buzzard in one of them. But the birds I saw did not look like the cartoonist draws them in the cartoon.

They didn't seem as filled with personality. In fact they looked like a beautiful black bird, not the wiseguy of the cartoons.

"The meshuginar dog won't recognize you in the new white truck," he said.

Usually when we get to the very end of Swan where it just turns into huge expanse of desert. That house at the very end, a meshuginar dog rushes out to bark at us and chase us. It gives me so much joy.

There are only a handful of houses along that whole long stretch. And each time I am on it I am so in love I say to Jim "if Bill was still here in Tucson, I'd want us to buy a house here. That one is a cute one."

They are all trailers. But fixed up nice. Living in a trailer is fine with me. I just love the beautiful desert out there. It is my favorite place.

It is Jim's least favorite. His favorite is the foothills. Which is the most desirable for everyone in Tucson, except for me. I love it out there in the beautiful empty desert where the buzzards hang out.

Because Jim informed me last week someone bought the abandoned Mervyns and the huge parking lot around it, and are digging up the parking lot now, I will never be able to go back there to brush up on my 3 point turn.

So when we got to the end of Swan Road, instead of making that little circle to go back, he said "why don't you practice your 3 point turn here." So I parked at the end. And I did it two times.

The motor went off a few times, I forgot stuff. And forgot about taking my foot off the clutch when I start in reverse, it bucked like crazy and made screeching noises.

I didn't think I did anything right, but for some reason Jim thought I did both times perfectly. He glowed. He was really proud of me.

The 3 point turn is a huge thing for the drivers test. Jim

knows they won't give me my license unless I can do it perfectly. He is totally involved in my 3 point turn.

I could care less about it right now. I really want with all my heart now just to learn how to drive, really drive, like a normal person.

Be able to get from here to there in Tucson. I want to be able to drive from house to the pool, to my market, to the things I go to.

I don't know if Jim and I have the same goals when we go driving out in the country.

When he wanted me to go to 4th gear almost right away on Corona Road I said "I don't want to go fast, I want to drink in the beauty."

And he said, "that is what we are here for, for you to learn your gears."

For me going to the countryside is all about having a wonderful time driving. And having a great time drinking in the beauty and seeing all the animals and birds.

It is all about giving Anne a glorious time. But for Jim it is serious driving lesson. In his mind all the time are the things he wants me to practice.

As a matter of fact before I even turned on Swan he wanted me to stay on Los Reales "so you can practice your wiggle waggle." Los Reales has a lot of steep curves as you near the end of it.

After doing my 3 point turn twice, it was too hot for the meshuginar dog to come out and rush me and bark his head off in glorious joy. It was really hot.

I said "I am going to drive to my dirt road now."

He said "why would you want to drive on all that dirt, it will mess up your beautiful new truck!"

But I am not going to give up driving on my dirt road. It is my only chance to drive as slow as I want and actually get to look around the whole time.

It is my favorite of everything.

And almost as soon as I turned on it I got a miracle. Jim didn't even see him. I saw him out my drivers window. It was a huge black bull. The blackest black I ever saw. And the beauty was a non pareil.

I had seen bulls before in that area. Sometimes a posse of them all together lying down. But mostly they were orange and white. I don't remember a black one. Altho one of the calves with them once was ebony black like this one. I guess he is his dad.

His beauty knocked me out. I instantly stopped the truck when I was a little past him. And then reversed to go back to get better view.

Jim didn't even see him till I pointed it out. "I want to go back but I don't want the noise of the truck to frighten him," I said.

Jim said "he's eating."

I guess there was tall grass there and he was snacking on it. So I only backed up a little way just so I could glimpse him. I didn't want to disturb him.

And I called loving endearments to him in soft crooning tone. And eventually his tail began to swish and then went around in a circle. He heard all my love talk.

Then I didn't want to irritate him so I put it back in first and slowly moved ahead still looking out the window at everything.

After that I did my U turn to go back. Because I discovered I was starving hungry and I knew Jim wanted me to do the wiggle waggle on Los Reales.

So I drove back along Swan to Los Reales. I remembered to signal when I was at the stop sign but I completely forgot to look and see if cars were coming. I found out too late that they were.

I had already pulled out and was making my turn when Jim called out "Not now! The cars are coming!"

Too late! I just kept going. But luckily nothing happened. I never did see those cars.

I guess all that driving on empty Swan Road and my beloved dirt road does not help me at all to remember what to do when I am not the only car on the road.

But there is nothing I can do about it. Whenever I am in the beautiful countryside I put my happiness first. That is all that matters to me. I'll just have to practice driving with other cars at another time, in another place.

My one concession to Jim was I was willing to drive to the end of Los Reales road, which does have quite a bit of traffic on it, or quite a bit for girl who has just driven with not a single other car.

I have no idea why he wants me to take those curves so fast. I would be willing to do it if I could see them coming up, see where they are, see where they lead. I like to see where I'm going.

But he doesn't like me to slow down.

"Speed up!" he said. "Go the speed limit!" he said. I did it to please him, but it stopped being relaxing driving for me. I just wanted it over with.

I did a beautiful U turn at the end. And Jim said "You drive back to Corona Road, we will return where we started. It's good for you to have a destination."

And I did. And then we switched seats.

I know I did something good in the lesson because there was one point when I finished Swan Road and was almost at Los Reales, when suddenly I saw my way clear.

I realized this is what driving is and if I keep practicing it, I actually will be a real driver. It is the first time I ever saw my way clear. Saw how it could happen to me, how I could actually be there.

Jim was tremendously excited after my lesson from the instant we switched seats and he began driving us home.

He is always tremendously excited after a lesson.

He is totally involved in the lesson. Everything that happened. What it means, what I can do, what I will do, what he will teach me to do.

He uses the whole ride home to give me further instruction. Pointing out everything he is doing while he is driving and explaining the reason for it.

I tune it all out. I don't listen to one word. I concentrate with my full mind and heart while I drive and instant I turn over the wheel to him, I want to completely forget about driving. I just want to kibitz and kid around.

I love kibitzing with Jim, I love to tease him.

"I'm older than you. I'm smarter than you. I'm better than you at everything," I say.

"I'm better than you at football, I'm better than you at driving. I took more drugs than you."

It's all malarkey beyond malarkey. I don't know football from a hole in the wall, and my drug career ended at age 30 when pot upset me instead of being the joy of my life.

Whereas Jim still buys pot from Pedro in south Tucson whenever he has the money to afford it.

Usually when I start up my malarkey with Jim, how I am better than he is at everything and how "he is lucky to have me for a friend so he has something to strive for," he always bites.

He can't not fall for it.

"Try not to be so jealous that I am better than you at everything," I say.

But no matter what I said on the way home from the lesson, and I kept upping the ante, there was nary a nibble. It fell on deaf ears. He would not be distracted.

All he wanted to talk about was my lesson and driving. He talked about driving the whole way home.

It was all instruction.

"See how I scooched up when I got near the light."

"Here I scooched up again."

He didn't even drive his usual way, as fast as he could to get where he's going fast.

All the cars on both sides were passing us. He was purposely going slower speed so I would pay attention to everything he was doing and then saying it to me too.

I couldn't get him off message for love or money. It lasted all the way till he pulled into my driveway. I didn't care. I just looked out the window and made appropriate responses. I was happy.

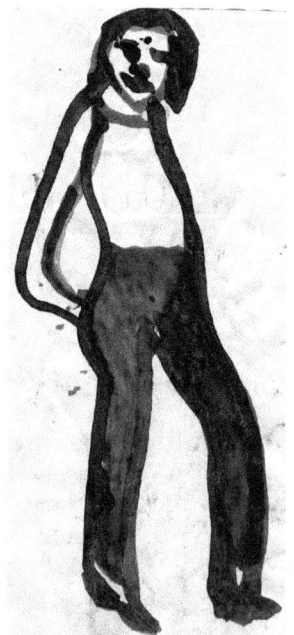

Pedro sells pot in south Tucson

July

Weather girls

Monsoon

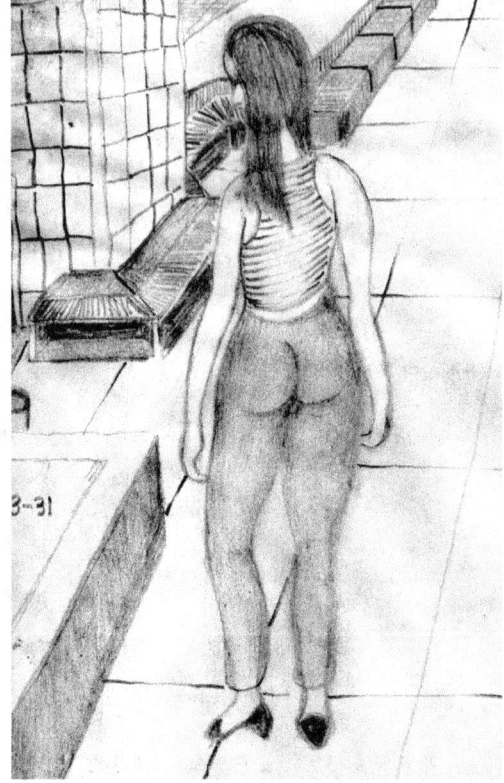

Waiting for the monsoons to come

Dawn is breaking and the birds woke up. I was up at first light, Priscilla came to get me.

I had already fed my kitties, put up my coffee, shut off the night lights in my house, sat at my computer, and was smoking a cigarette and drinking coffee when the birds woke up.

All their calls came at once. The throaty call of the morning dove. The high pitched chirping in nest. None has made an appearance yet. There is just the sound of them all being awake in their nests.

There is a lot more light in the sky now than there was when I first opened my eyes. It is thrilling dawn breaking, there is no way around that. It all seems like miracles. I open my eyes and the light in the sky is barely discernible. It is the very start of dawn.

Fifteen minutes later you hear the first bird calls. The light has grown. And now 20 minutes later there is enuf light that I can clearly see my cat Cupcake playing in her yard.

Daylight has started. It is no longer light first arising in a night sky. It is the beginning of day light. There is no more night.

A new day has begun.

Monsoon season started yesterday. Clouds filled the sky. The air turned dense. The idea of rain and thunder and lightning came back into my mind. The night air was warm instead of cool.

Monsoon season begins off with waiting for it to arrive. I

guess that is miraculous too, almost as miraculous as dawn breaking.

A monsoon is a huge thing. It means a huge storm blows into Tucson with majestic thunder, electrical skies, and the blessing of rain.

A monsoon is a very big storm and very welcomed by all desert dwellers. The earth, the plants, the animals, the humans.

Monsoons turn us all into one being. The earth, the trees, the animals, the humans, we become one being waiting for our lover to arrive. The monsoon is our lover.

It's all so royal. That huge clash of thunder taking over our endless sky. Lightning is so far out there are no words for it. Monsoons are always electrical storms, huge electrical storms.

For some reason rain is not a given. It is what we all want most in the whole world. The entire desert is treated to the lightning, the thunder. It all takes place as far as the eye can see, as far as the ear can hear, but rain seems to be another story.

Someone somewhere always gets rain and you hope it will be you. But the rain can fall anywhere. It can fall on the other side of the mountain, or to the west of you, the east of you, the north of you, the south of you.

The rain doesn't always come to Tucson. And even when it does, a town sprawled out on the desert this way, it takes a miracle for it to arrive in your own backyard.

The next morning after a monsoon, everyone in Tucson who got rain asks everyone else they see "Did you get the rain?"

And we either answer "YES!! Wasn't it great."

Or "No, did you? Where did it rain?"

LOL a monsoon which doesn't bring rain to your neck of the woods is like a lot of intense foreplay. Hot sex which goes on for hours. And then no climax, no release.

And the next afternoon at around 4 pm it starts all over again. The first streak of lightning in the sky, the first rumble of thunder. And hours and hours of all that intense foreplay.

It is like that day after day for weeks on end. Sometimes you get the amazing satisfaction of great long drenching rain.

Pounding rain. The rain never lasts long. It is way too pounding too forceful to be a long lasting rain. At best a monsoon rain is ten minutes.

But what a rain! What a release! What an experience!

And the intense gratitude, that it resulted in rain, not the frustration of the previous week.

I'm just saying monsoons are a hot and heavy love affair with the desert. They arrive every year around July 4th and stick around for about 6 weeks.

But as Sam, the head lifeguard at Fort Lowell pool said to me 3 years ago, "They start off with so much force, all that incredible amazing energy, and by the end they are depleted. Halfway thru monsoon season they are not what they were when they first arrived."

But today is the first day of anticipating their arrival. It may take two weeks for them to arrive in Tucson.

July 5th

Insight

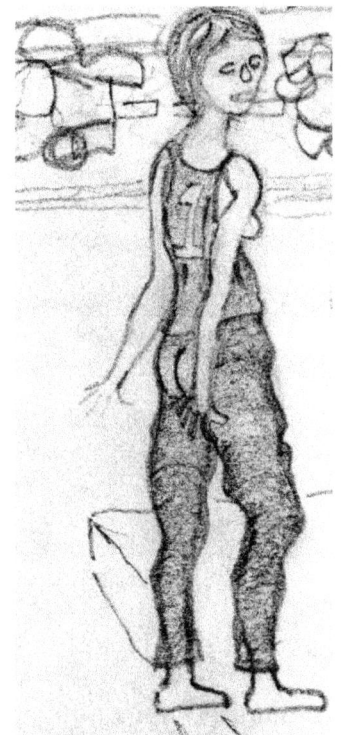

She turns a corner

It's a beautiful morning. A woodlands morning. It rained for two days. The earth is wet and spongy. The leaves are green. The sky still has a few wet clouds in it. And the world out there is still dripping wet. New born and dripping wet.

The hell of relentless heat without a drop of water has ended. I don't know how we withstood it. We didn't withstand it. It drove us straight around the bend.

That last afternoon before the rain finally came in the middle of the night, that last afternoon two days ago, I sat here at my desk comatose looking out the window.

Searching the sky for rain clouds. The weather channel had promised rain that day. But it was 4:30 in the afternoon, hot as hell, dry as dust, nothing in the whole wide world was stirring. The sun was glaring as usual and not a cloud in the sky.

The girl was hopeless and desperate and could not move a muscle. Not a thought stirred in her head. She just sat at her desk looking out her open window at her hot stifling dried up desert backyard.

Rain seemed like a fairy tale. She no more believed it would actually rain than she believed there would be knock at her door and a lovely prince would say "I've been looking for you far and wide and now I have found you."

And take her to a tiny little palace in the woods with her very own lake. And she would swim with the fishes and think "fairy tales do come true."

I think Anne needed rescuing. It wasn't only the world around her which was unbearable, that was the least of it really. It was that the world inside her head was unbearable.

It was unbearable living inside her own mind. It was like a stifling pressure vise. Not a thought stirred. She couldn't move a muscle, she couldn't move a thought.

"What is it?" she finally asked her Higher Self.

"You're miserable," her Higher Self answered.

And that helped, hearing the bald truth.

And then that night while she was sleeping the rain came. Her prince came and delivered her. That's really what the rain was. Tucson was the damsel in distress and the rain was our prince charming. He swept in from the west and delivered us.

He gave us back our life. To the earth and the trees and the animals and the people.

We could contemplate life starting up again. It didn't start up again right away. We were all saved but we were still blitzed out from what we had been thru.

It rained all the next day too, yesterday. And this morning finally life feels normal again. I had forgotten what normal was. I had forgotten what feeling normal was.

It had been so long in that abnormality that normal just became a refreshing dream, but ephemeral— does it exist? did it ever exist? what is it? will it ever happen again? Am I going to be stuck in this loop forever.

And yet here it is. Right before me, right inside me. What is as wonderful as normal. Nothing. My yard is normal, I am normal, my kitties are normal, the birds flying around are normal.

The world awoke from its crazy dream, we are all normal again. The blessed relief of feeling normal again.

Of being out of that airless stifling high-pressure place. Without that crushing intensity.

Normal is so simple and natural and real. It simply means life is not hell. It is lovely. It is made up of movement, it has flow, it has bounce. It is not a constant call for deliverance, you are delivered. You are free. Your life has been restored to you.

Anne has an insight

I slept on and off all yesterday. I didn't undertake anything. I was blitzed. I just listened to the rain with satisfaction. I watched the rain with satisfaction and then went back to TV and went back to sleep.

Just a little TV and a lot of naps. 10 minutes of TV and

fall sleep for another hour.

TV couldn't hold me, it didn't interest me. I would get up and go to my computer. But nothing was happening there either. Back to TV for another attempt and fall sleep for another hour.

I would be waiting for show to come on and when I woke up the show was over.

And then in the evening to my great surprise I had two big breakthroughs. The first was when I first opened my eyes from a dream about my high school boyfriend.

We had stayed good friends till 10 years ago when suddenly out of nowhere for no reason at all he dropped me like a hot potato. He never answered my phone calls. I never heard from him again.

And in the dream I was with him again, not as boyfriend and girlfriend as we had been in high school, but as the good friends we had been our whole adult life.

And when I woke up I had such a longing for him. A longing to be with him again, to have his friendship back in my life. A longing for him.

And I thought about the longing. What is it I longed for so much? And it seemed like it was the atmosphere of him. I just wanted his atmosphere back in my life. I longed for it acutely.

I don't even know what an atmosphere is. But it is the only word which came into my mind to describe what it is I longed for.

And then I realized I had spent these past two weeks, this whole trying time, of longing for everything. Of longing for my brother, my cousin, all my old friends, everyone who had ever been in my life, everyone I had ever been close to.

It had been two weeks of total longing. And suddenly the most amazing thought entered my mind.

The New Age teaches that everyone out there (everyone in your life who you experience as out there, outside yourself) isn't really out there, isn't really outside yourself.

They are all part of you that you see outside yourself. Each is a portion of you that you have projected out there.

And suddenly what occurred to me is maybe I am longing for the whole of my self.

After all there must be a much greater self, a huge self, if it includes every single person out there.

And it is not specific people I am longing for, my old high school boyfriend, my cousin, my family, my old friends from New York City. Each one of them carries some part of me. A self that I am unaware of and only experience as out there in someone else.

And what I am longing for with all my heart is myself. I want myself back.

Somehow for some reason I got rid of myself and only experience it as out there in others. And now I want my self back. I want myself.

That is why the longing is so acute and so constant and won't go away and why I can't ever get any satisfaction.

I keep hoping they will call me or write me or try to contact me. Connect up with me again. I want my connection with them back.

But each time I try all I experience is their absence. They are all completely absent in my life. They were there and now they are absent. They've all totally lost interest in me.

It is a conundrum I haven't been able to get around. Why were they interested in me then, but disinterested in me now. How could I have totally lost interest for everyone I have ever known and loved.

But when I woke up last evening to that longing for my old highschool boyfriend, for his friendship in my life, and it seemed what I wanted was his atmosphere. His presence in my life. Just what he emitted. Just to be around him. To have him close and near and be a part of me again.

I knew then, it simply struck me, that it had to be my Self I was longing for. That each one of these people hold a part of myself. And I want them all back because I am longing for my Self again.

I just knew it was true. It was the only thing which made sense out of everything. Nothing else did.

And then I knew two things. I knew that this terrible time of intensity, which I had experienced as so unbearable. Stress on one side, and emptiness and longing on the other.

That it all had a purpose and its purpose was to bring me to this point. Its purpose was for me to grow. To reach a point in my consciousness which is higher than it was before it all began.

And the growth meant realizing I do have a greater Self and it is that greater self that I want so desperately now. That I want to be in contact with and get to know. Be in my life, have in my life, interact with in my life.

I don't remember my second insight. I don't remember when I had it. I don't remember what it was. But I know it too was a greater understanding. New way of seeing and understanding. Of seeing from a higher place.

July 20

Jim and I take Alice to lunch on her birthday

My friend Alice is intrepid

Yesterday was Alice's birthday so Jim and I took her out to lunch. It was good teamwork on our part. I am the one who remembered when Alice's birthday was and had the idea we would take her to lunch.

But Jim and Alice are such old and close friends. They have both been at Racquet Club forever and were probably good friends there before I even moved to Tucson. And speak on the phone with each other almost every day too.

When Alice invited us both to her house for Thanksgiving last November, it all took place on email between me and Alice.

Jim is not on email. Which meant I had to call Jim when I got the email inviting us. Then I had to call him again when I got the email asking what time do we get hungry.

Since Jim was going to drive me there, Alice would email me with her question. I would call Jim to get the answer. Then I would email Alice back.

It was all so round about and I was monkey in the middle.

This time it was so simple and I did not have to do a thing.

Plus I did not have to deal with Jim's resistance. He is not a social butterfly. Every year he is invited to 5 Thanksgivings and manages to get out of all of them. He grew up in Tucson and all his family is still here. Beside his cousins and their families, he has nieces and nephew and their families.

He is invited to 3 Thanksgivings in Tucson and two up in Phoenix where his best friend from childhood lives and invites him to his family Thanksgiving.

When I realized Thanksgiving was coming up and it was my first Thanksgiving without Bill, I thought maybe Jim and I could go to a restaurant in the neighborhood together to have a nice meal.

But when I said in the car "what are you doing for Thanksgiving?" He said "**nothing!**" loud and clear.

He was so adamant. I realize now it was because he didn't want me to try to trap him into Thanksgiving. He likes to just stay home with his cat and watch football.

But I didn't know that then. I just knew that he didn't have any plans for Thanksgiving and didn't want any.

But when Alice emailed and invited us I instantly delightedly wrote back "yes."

I couldn't go without him driving me. And if I was aware then of how much he just wanted to stay home with his cat and watch football, I ignored it.

I simply insisted we go to Alice's for Thanksgiving. Because I wanted it with all my heart. My family was Jewish, we didn't have Christmas dinner or Easter dinner or New Years dinner.

All we had was Thanksgiving. And it was a huge deal and I always loved it. It is the only American holiday we celebrated.

Jim was gracious enough to take me to Thanksgiving at Alice's house. And I did have a wonderful time. And it did mean a great deal to me.

But from the instant we got home and every day afterward he said "next year you have to drive yourself to Alice's for Thanksgiving." He aint going. He wants his cat, his football, and to be home.

"Fine" I said. "I'll drive myself." We are both assuming that I will know how to drive by then. (He did have a nice time but it is not how he likes to spend Thanksgiving.)

But I was very aware of when Alice's birthday was because last year Jim told me "Alice is going to the Bob Dylan concert on her birthday." And I knew how much it meant to Alice.

And when the clouds got really dark at the time her concert began I worried it would be rained out. She had been looking forward to it and excited about it for a week from what Jim had told me.

And the next morning I emailed Alice asking her about it. And she said they had gone out to dinner before hand. And she ordered margarita cheese cake. And how wonderful and miraculous the concert was.

It hadn't rained but an incredible misty glow lit up with radiant sun behind it arrived during the violin solo. Alice was transported.

And then instant she got home that miraculous blessed rain arrived. So Alice had gotten everything. She got taken to dinner on her birthday. She loved the Bob Dylan concert she had treated herself to. And she did not miss out on the blessed rain. She was happy lassie and had best birthday ever.

So I knew how much celebrating her birthday meant to her.

And almost immediately afterward I said to Jim "if she has no other plans for her birthday next year, let's take her out to lunch.

"I will treat both you and Alice. You can order whatever you want."

I said "Come on, it will be easy for you. We can have lunch at the restaurant at the Racquet Club, you don't have to go anywhere."

And when I said that, he agreed. He likes the food at the Racquet Club restaurant and treats himself to lunch there sometimes. So that was the plan for almost a year.

Until last month when he began telling me there is a

place near Racquet Club which makes good pizza. And of course I'm dying for pizza.

In Tucson I get fast food Mexican take-out all the time, but I haven't had pizza in 10 years. And I love pizza, who doesn't!

So I said "let's go for pizza on Alice's birthday."

And by some happy miracle he took it all into his own hands. A week before her birthday he called her and said we want to take her lunch. And he reported back to me she was excited.

That was a good sign. "Let's go for pizza" I said.

He said "it's her birthday she chooses the restaurant."

"Great!" I said. I was curious which restaurant she will choose.

I was sure I memorized the date right. For 6 months I had been saying to Jim in the car "we will take Alice out to lunch on her birthday on July 17th."

And 2 weeks ago I said "July 17th is a Tuesday, that is when we have Alice's birthday lunch."

And on the Monday before it, I said "tomorrow we take Alice out to lunch for her birthday, which restaurant did she choose?"

And he said "I just talked to her. Her birthday is

Thursday."

"O" I said, "O."

So I switched it all in my mind. "Thursday we take Alice out for lunch for her birthday, not tomorrow."

It turned out the day I thought was her birthday she was driving to Bisbee to see her friends.

And then day before her real birthday, on late Wednesday afternoon, Jim called.

He said "she wants to go to the Tucson art museum for her birthday lunch. It is all the way downtown."

He arranged with Alice they meet at Racquet Club, then she drives with him to pick me up at Y after my swim, and she will drive us there.

And then back to Racquet Club when it is over, where my truck will be, and he will drive us home.

I couldn't understand the why of this arrangement. Jim drops me off for my swim and continues on to Racquet Club for his swim, and then drives us both home. He lives just a few blocks away from me.

But when I started to ask questions about the arrangement, it was clear it was what he wanted, so I said "fine."

And then I started to get excited about it. Alice had come

up with such a good idea. We would be having lunch in the art museum. Way downtown. I started to get thrilled. And planned what I would buy at the museum gift shop.

And I liked it that it wasn't just pizza or chinese food in a neighborhood restaurant. Something interesting, unusual and exotic for me.

It was fun being picked up by Jim and Alice in Alice's car when I finished my swim yesterday.

And Jim got out of passenger seat and sat in back so I could watch Alice drive. Alice is great driver and a great teacher, I thought I would learn things.

But I only paid attention for a little while because then I got interested in listening to her conversation.

As soon as we got there I understood everything. The restaurant is not in the art museum as I imagined. Maybe it is behind it or very near it.

All the way down there Alice had raved about it and said it is her favorite restaurant. The food is so delicious and the price is so reasonable.

Both appealed to me. I love delicious food and since I was paying for it I was happily surprised it would not be an arm and a leg.

Also I understood why the arrangement was made that

Alice drive us there. Alice has been in an art show in every single building in downtown Tucson. She knows downtown Tucson like the back of her hand.

She knew exactly how to find this little restaurant, A La Carte, which is her favorite restaurant in the whole world. The food is so delicious and price is so reasonable. And she loves the plants and the mosaics.

But never in a million years would Jim have been able to find it on his own. It really is tucked away and behind things. Maybe behind the art museum.

And to reach it you have to wind thru many teeny streets, none of which Alice could remember the name of. She just goes there by heart.

When she reached the last tiny street she looked up and said "Myers! That is the name of the street. I couldn't remember its name."

So I realized that at first Alice had given Jim directions so we would all meet there, but it had proved impossible. Too many tiny streets with names Alice could not remember.

The parking lot was filled but Alice knew she could park on the street outside it, which we did.

When we were leaving Jim pointed out to me it would

have taken him an hour to find the place. It would have been frustrating. And then an hour to figure out where to park.

I understood perfectly. It made tremendous good sense that Alice would drive us there and back to Racquet Club when it was over to pick up the truck.

I had resisted the idea when Jim first told me about it because I said "why do we have to drive all the way north to Racquet Club when we could just shoot right home when lunch is over?"

But absolutely it's the perfect idea. Whoever came up with it, Alice or Jim, is genius.

The restaurant was not fancy. It was homey, a place you could be very comfortable. It really was a café.

We passed a beautiful stone sculpture of man and woman kissing, we must have been right behind the art museum. And then walked into patio of the restaurant.

I instantly loved the patio. There were big umbrellas over every table to protect from the heat. And it was ringed with wonderful green shrubbery and all the birds.

I knew instantly that I wanted to eat outside there so I could smoke my head off plus be outside.

Inside was crowded, we had arrived exactly at lunch

hour. You wait on that line to tell her what you want, and then she brings it to you.

I didn't want to be in there altho it was such an appealing place. I wanted to be outside and have a cigarette.

So I handed Jim my credit card. I said "order for me whatever Alice orders for herself. Tell Alice she can have whatever she wants in the whole world.

"Let's sit outside. Then I can smoke my cigarettes and you can smoke your cigars."

Jim loves air conditioning, he hates heat. But he also likes to smoke his cigars so he agreed.

So I did not wait on line with them to give my order. I was able to rush right back outside and light a cigarette.

No one else was eating outside, altho inside it was crowded.

I could choose any table I wanted so I chose one at the end. Near that wonderful stone sculpture of the lovers and right by the gorgeous green shrubbery and all the plants. I was very happy there.

They came out. Jim lit his cigar. I lit another cigarette and offered Alice one of mine. She rolls her own to save money.

And then a lovely time was had by all.

Jim worried when it took so long for them to bring the food that they wouldn't know we were out there. We were the only ones.

But eventually the food did come and he was crazy about his hamburger and french fries. They were delicious. "It's a good hamburger," he kept saying.

And whatever Alice and I had was delicious too. And the waitress arrived with 3 tall glasses of delicious home-made lemonade for all of us. On ice.

And the sandwich was on delicious home made bread. With a lovely salad side. And cantaloupe on the side. Delicious cantaloupe. And the sandwich was scrumptious.

It was all home made and delicious. Just as Alice had said. "Real food" she kept saying. And she is right. Alice is a chef and she knows." Whoever does their cooking for them is a real chef," she said. And she is right.

"What's the name of this place?" Jim asked her. "A la Carte" she said. And I knew he asked because he liked it and maybe would return.

I was too excited to take more than a few bites of my lunch. I was happy smoking cigs and drinking that delicious lemonade.

Jim and Alice polished off their lunch and loved every morsel. I was just happy being there with them.

Conversation was a joy because I am such close friends with Jim. Alice is such close friends with him. And he is so comfortable and happy with both of us.

No one had to strain to make sure everyone fitted in and was included. It was almost like family in that way, or cousins, not like socializing.

We are all so deeply familiar with each other and there is so much genuine affection. And we are so relaxed with each other.

Jim and I did tease each other, but I told Alice all the jokes so she would be let in and could join in the teasing. So the 3 of us could have fun and silliness and not have grown up conversation..

And then Alice's cell phone rang and it turned out to be her son in North Carolina wishing her happy birthday. And I am sure it made him happy to hear his mom is at a restaurant being treated to birthday lunch by her friends.

And all his news made Alice glow. He is the business manager of something. And he told Alice he is going to New York.

Alice was delighted because her other son is there. "The

whole family will be together," she said with so much joy.

And he told Alice he is going to India.

"India!" She was so surprised. And happy. "They have beautiful material there, bring me back some material. And send me a postcard."

Then he said, after that he is going to Malaysia.

"Malaysia!" she said so surprised. "They have sapphires there." Alice makes jewelry. "At least send me a postcard, please send me postcards."

It was just such a joy listening to Alice's side of the conversation. She was so clearly happy to be talking to him. There was so much love in her voice. So much love and happiness.

She called him endearments. I never heard Alice use an endearment. She called him honey. And she was so pleased with all his news. "I am proud of you," she said.

And she was so happy to be proud of her son, and I knew he was so happy to hear that.

Gosh in my whole life I never heard either of my parents say to me "I am proud of you honey."

As much as me and Jim and Alice were enjoying our birthday lunch, I really think it was that phone call which lit it all up for Alice.

It was a mother's dream come true of a phone call and on her birthday! Alice is a world traveler. She has lived in the Mid East and in Turkey. And all those years in Mexico. She loved it that her son would be in India and Malaysia.

She really wanted those postcards tho. She did say "Be sure to send me postcards."

Then I said "Alice don't you want cappuccino and dessert."

She said "yes."

I said "I'll go in and order it for you. Which dessert do you want?"

She said "I like the ones they have on the top shelf with apricot."

I thought the price for the cappuccino and pastry was an incredible bargain. And when she brought the cappuccino and pastry out to Alice, the cappuccino was enormous. Big enough for 3 people.

Alice drank some of it but who could finish it! And had some of her delicious pastry but said she was too full from her lunch.

And the girl brought Alice out a container to pour in the rest of her cappuccino to have on the way home and container for her pastry.

And I got a container to take my sandwich home and my side.

And I asked her if we could have refills on our lemonade and she did.

And then Alice's friend from Racquet Club called to wish her happy birthday. And I heard Alice say "I will take a swim before I go home."

So it seemed like the perfect time to close out the party. I asked our waitress for a drink container so I could sip on my lemonade on the way home.

And Jim thought it wasn't fair of me to make her work so much. For her to go back in and get it for me after she had already brought Alice her containers.

But I was so appreciative and grateful and said "it is Alice's birthday."

And then when we got to the car I realized I had left my pretty bag with the books I had written under the table.

I had thought we were going to the art museum and was going to give them to the girls who worked at the counter at the gift shop.

But I didn't want to go back and get it. "I hope the waitresses find it and read the books," I said to Jim.

And then Alice drove us back to Racquet Club. And she

really thanked both me and Jim in the parking lot.

I had brought two pretty sundresses as a gift to Alice. And even tho the birthday present her twin sister had given her was a skirt made out of bamboo, it was the loveliest softest material I ever felt.

Still it was long and very dark brown, not summery at all. And the blouse Alice had worn with it to brighten it up was long sleeved and did not look cool.

"Change into your sundress after your swim," I told Alice, "so you have something cool to wear."

When we talked about New York at the table. Alice did live in New York City for quite a while altho she grew up in Syracuse. I guess she came to New York when she finished art school.

And she married there and had her first son there. She had her second son when she was living in Mexico and married to a Mayan.

Jim is really curious about New York and wants to spend some time there.

So Alice said all the things about New York. "You can go ice skating at Rockefeller Center" she said.

She told me and Jim when she was a small child her mother had taken her to New York City and they visited

Rockefeller Center. A man was painting a mural.

Alice was a little girl but she told him "I am an artist too." And he let her paint in the flag. And then he invited her to have picnic lunch with him and his wife next to it.

She said they tore down the mural tho because he had put in the pig.

Apparently Rockefeller had commissioned the mural and he had painted Rockefeller as a pig.

It took a while to dawn on me that it was Diego Rivera and his wife Frida Kahlo. That Diego Rivera had let Alice paint in the flag on his mural. It was a small flag.

But they had torn down Diego Rivera's mural with Alice's flag in it.

I immediately turned to Jim. "When you go to New York and meet a girl you like, first you invite her out for cappuccino and a cannoli.

"And if that mural were still up you would take your girl to Rockefeller Center after your cappuccino and cannoli. And point to the flag and say your friend in Tucson painted it with Diego Rivera and Frida Kahlo. And the girl will jump into bed with you."

"I can't believe you had lunch with Diego Rivera and Frida Kahlo!" I said to Alice. "Wow!"

"And now she is having lunch with us," Jim said.

I busted out laughing. "She sure has come down in the world," I giggled.

But a girl can do worse than having lunch with me and Jim.

Jim behave yourself in New York City
There are some wild wimmin there

The end
Tucson Arizona
July 21, 2012

Coming attractions

The year 2012 is half over
Let's see what the rest of this year brings us
All my love to you
From Anne, Priscilla and Cupcake

An open letter to anyone who wants to write or even dreams of doing it

Go for it!
Writing is easy and fun
Here is my experience

November is National Write a Novel in a Month and a month before November '08, my friend Lisa in Tucson told me about it, and suggested I do it. But I was used to writing short stories and posting them on my Blog (the stories are mostly about my yesterday)— I never wrote a novel and didn't know how.

So I just wrote polite thank you back to Lisa.

But thank God she pushed me. Because when November 3rd rolled around, I decided to give it a try. And to my big surprise, I loved doing it.

I just went to my machine when I woke up with cup of coffee and pack of cigarettes, and wrote for 45 minutes each morning for 3 straight weeks. I still spent my afternoons and evenings posting on current events forum.

I was doing it for a week when Lisa encouraged me to register at the site (NANO) (it is free) and then I received their pep-talk emails, which they sent out to everyone.

Lisa was doing it too, even tho she had never written in her life, she is a painter.

But this is a great way for anyone who has ever dreamed of being a writer to do it. Every November there is another one. I hope you consider doing it too. All you have to do is write for 45 minutes each day for month of November. No editing! No re-writing!

You can begin by telling about your yesterday too, but after you have done that several times, start to write a story which is long enough to hold your interest to keep telling it for a while.

(Telling a story means "and then" "and then" "and then." First this happened, then that happened, then that happened, then that happened.)

This will give you experience in narrative (telling a story) and there is very good chance that in the middle you will "find your own voice."

This means right in the middle of telling your story, suddenly you hear a voice in your head dictating a different story.

This one is about your earliest childhood, it is all things you have forgotten, and the voice is different, it is in the first person (even if you have been writing in 3rd person) and it is very personal. And you will love it!

If this happens, immediately stop writing what you were writing, and instead start writing everything you are hearing.

This is called "finding your own voice" as a writer, it makes writing so easy and fun, you just take down what it says— or as they say "you get out of the way, and the story writes itself."

That is the way I became a writer back in NYC. I was in my late 20s then and had just been fired from my job. Bill was working as Wall Street messenger then for $96/week. He said "why don't you become a writer, I will support you." I thought it was a great idea, I decided to do it.

So I wrote three tiny 2 page stories about my yesterday and then sat down to write long story, I wrote it in 3rd person and it was about a love affair before I met my husband. That topic interested me enough to keep telling the story.

But right in the middle of it, I was a few weeks into it, I heard that voice dictating a whole other story. It was my littlest little girl experiences.

It is the same as learning how to balance on a bicycle.

One day they are supporting you, and you are pedaling, and then suddenly out of nowhere, you balance. You can ride a bike.

You never thought it would happen to you, even tho you watched all your friends do it, because it looks like magic.

It is the same way with writing. You push yourself along telling a story, and then suddenly you balance. You hear that voice and simply take down what it says. The story writes itself, you get out of the way.

But you can only learn how to balance on a bike when you are on a bike, and you can only hear your own voice, while you are at the machine writing. But it is as natural and effortless as learning how to balance on a bike. It comes to all.

Guess what! CreateSpace owned by Amazon publishes any book written by anyone for free, but you have to do all the work yourself. No one even reads it.

You have to format it for a paperback book, all they do is press a button to print and bind it, and post it for sale on Amazon.

When I saw the technical work involved in formatting my novel into a paperback book I was terrified. I didn't even know what they were talking about or how to do any of it.

But I was too deep into it to quit. I wanted to publish my novel now, I didn't just want it lost on my computer.

It turns out CreateSpace has community boards. And there are angels on it (people who have published lots and lots of books, are completely experienced) and they walk us newbies thru everything. Ones even less experienced than me, they wrote their book and don't even know how to indent a paragraph or what a tab is or how to edit.

It turned out everything which seemed impossibly hard when I first heard about it, is not hard, you just press a button in your word processing program.

But of course I needed to learn from the community boards which button? where? things like that. They have the patience of saints there and love to help.

I tell you all this because it is God's gift to writers. That we can publish ourselves. CreateSpace also does videos, and music, photography books, art books, comic books.

Lulu does this too. It was first started by Lulu.com. Everyone at CreateSpace started there. Both places are wonderful and many publish at both places. Both Lulu and CreateSpace are free, they publish your book for free and post it on Amazon. A gift from Heaven to all artists.

I tell you all this to encourage you to go for it! If I could do it anyone can. Before I began writing I was convinced I didn't have a creative bone in my body.

I had always loved writing book reports and compositions for school, and always loved writing letters. But I was never artistic in anyway.

Because it turns out it is all there under the surface for everyone. But you have to be willing to give it a whirl for it to emerge. There is no such thing as talent. It is only when you are actually doing it, that interesting and surprising things happen.

Writing is a big treat you give yourself, because it is way to get to know yourself.

It is never too late to start. Whenever you do is the perfect time. And there is nothing to compare with the freshness of your early beginning.

So think of starting writing, as like the beginning of Spring. Later you will develop more skills, but there is nothing like the beginning. When all the miracles, freshness and inspiration happen.

I wish you luck on your enterprise!

I love you, Anne

Thank you Helen Kritzler

Because no one can publish a book without help, I am deeply grateful to Helen Kritzler for doing all the book covers for my books. It is a huge favor.

Here is her own drawing of girl stubbing her toe. I like it so much I asked her to put it on back cover of my first novel *Ruthie Has a New Love.*

*Aww I stubbed my toe
drawing by Helen Kritzler*

Other books by Anne Wilensky

Novels

Ruthie Has a New Love

Girl Blog From Tucson

MORE Girl Blog From Tucson

Sweet Sound of Bird Song
a momentous year in Anne's life

History

Not what you'd expect
How the women's liberation movement started
My personal experience of it
Published 2011

Anne Wilensky books published by Haiku Helen Press
Bill's cartoons are at billstampone.blogspot.com